Charlotte Elwood is an Australian author whose life story is as captivating as the tales she weaves. Born into the challenges of poverty, she exemplifies resilience, determination, and the unwavering pursuit of knowledge. Charlotte's sense of adventure, hope, and boundless curiosity have driven her to explore the darkest corners of humanity's stories, shedding light on the misunderstood and marginalized. With a heart as kind as it is diligent, she embodies the belief that even the most challenging circumstances can fuel the brightest aspirations for the future.

To my dearest Emma,

In the vast narrative of my life, you have been the guiding star, the hope behind every chapter. Your love, support, and unwavering belief in my dreams have illuminated the darkest corners of my journey, infusing each moment with purpose and possibility. With boundless gratitude and endless love, I dedicate this story and all its triumphs to you, my muse and my heart's true home.

Charlotte Elwood

PANDEMONIUM

AUSTIN MACAULEY PUBLISHERS™
LONDON • CAMBRIDGE • NEW YORK • SHARJAH

The right of Charlotte Elwood to be identified as the author of this work has been asserted by the author in accordance with sections 77 and 78 of the Copyright, Designs and Patents Act 1988.

A CIP catalogue record for this title is available from the British Library.

ISBN 9781528901055 (Paperback)
ISBN 9781528907002 (Hardback)
ISBN 9781528916400 (ePub e-book)
ISBN 9781528915663 (Audiobook)

www.austinmacauley.co.uk

First Published 2024
Austin Macauley Publishers Ltd®
1 Canada Square
Canary Wharf
London
E14 5AA

To those whose support became the bedrock of my journey, I extend my deepest gratitude. In moments where perseverance and strength faltered, you stood as pillars of encouragement. Your belief in me fueled the flame of determination, turning challenges into stepping stones and dreams into reality. To my steadfast companions on this literary odyssey, your presence has been the most cherished gift. This book stands as a testament to our collective resilience, shared triumphs, and the boundless power of a supportive community. Thank you for being the wind beneath my wings; this achievement is as much yours as it is mine.

Chapter 1

Rape. Blood. Gore. Insanity. A bright red hue in the eyes of its people. The land has engulfed itself. The innocent is threatened by the ever-growing thirst of its individuals for power. The year 3120 has just passed, and the world is in chaos. The fact is that all that is true is the life we live now. The system we live in now. It does not matter what you existed as before. All that matters is that society now doesn't exist like that anymore. Clicks, clichés and social angst are still the same but the social status quo that once was? Gone.

It all started when Theodoris took control – a powerful coup on our world that we were not prepared for. Luckily, this continent was one of the last to be seized, even though the provocateur had already penetrated all levels of government ranks and enlisted in most of our army. This was a mechanism that was imposed. It was all the armed forces could do after the Enzonians, a somewhat mega-force tried to take over the world through the use of nuclear weapons and violent force. But because of the Theodoris's conscription and training for warriorship at such young ages, it was only natural that they were recruited everywhere to fight the Enzonians. No one knew what devastation was to come though. But those were early days. Soon enough, radical extremists fought back in revolt and rapidly there was nothing left but ruins of our former society. The Enzonians were abolished but a new, far greater, threat evolved, on the Continent, in the birth of the Razors. These were traditionally rebels who rose up against the Theodoris in the hope of maintaining order; only superseded by the psychopaths who evolved within them. Trade moved from capitalism to power through warfare. We declined as a civilisation back to the early days of tribes and no one could be trusted, especially when torture and sadistic forms of government were involved. Darwinism is the only true thing that remains. Well, that's our truth anyway.

The world itself, overtaken by dense undergrowth and forests, makes for good hiding spots and places to deploy traps, but it also does the exact same for the Razors. Once invaded by them, you almost never survive. I only know because I am what they call a wanderer. They think I have no grounding, no place to level myself, which is untrue. Our home is the scrub; especially when to be settlers, taking root in one place leaves you vulnerable to falling victim to an ambush. Murdered, extorted and bound to slavery in every way possible, that's why we wander. Besides, there aren't too many places left that allow secrecy.

My band of sisters and brothers have seen enough to know to avoid strangers, as they could be scouts in disguise. They are recruiting them young. Even a two-year-old can find a base camp and become the catalyst for the destruction of the Settler's colony; which the Razors cause.

Razors use torture, oppression, and rape; they dominate people in ways that you can only imagine in nightmares. The Settlers' children watch on, only to inevitably be desensitised to the whole scene, and in time they too become Razors. Even the women Razors were compassionless to the point that they were participating in the fucking and torturing of other men and women. This was their way of controlling us, through fear of mutilation or worse. Horrifically, some captives survive the onslaught, only to later become 'lucky' enough to be kept as pets. I was one of those.

My camp, a relatively small pacifist settlement hidden amongst the central mountains, was invaded when I was young. We had many governing rules from the old world to keep our settlement safe. One of these involved arms, and if you weren't at the watchtower or hunting for food, you weren't allowed guns. Weapons were purposeful. My father used to teach us the use of a gun and other components when we went out hunting. How to aim, the art of tracking and trapping and the never-ending patience involved. One day we were hunting a padymelon and he said to me, "Patience is a virtue." Something they used to say in the old world. Followed by, "Sweetheart, sometimes it's a game of who can stand to be still the longest." And we would wait in the lush colourful undergrowth of the lacy ferns. At first, hunting didn't come naturally to me. I would wriggle and complain and spoil the stalk. I didn't comprehend why it was important. But as I grew, my father's words and the status of the hunt for the game became implicit. I had a revelation that the survival of the community is vital in comparison to my own individual need for comfort.

Our downfall came when a baby was found by one of our female food gatherers, crying in the dense undergrowth of the nearby forest. The Razors were cunning and had placed it there as a trap. Being a small country, the majority of guns had been taken by the then Theodoris's government and were hard to come by, so we were easy pickings for the Razors. I remember the watchtower men shouting and my mum and dad yelling at us to get inside our tent. I fear we were already trapped from the outside in. My brother, Chase, and I hugged close and as he wrapped himself around me, he covered my ears to protect me from the scene unfolding before us. Guns went off and there was plenty of shouting until everyone was rallied into the centre of our site. I searched my father's bearded face for any expression of where to go next, but he was fixated on one person. A tall, muscular man with fair hair and a look like that of a tiger on a battlefield. The leader yelled commands with authority, "Get on your knees! Don't fucken move! Keep your head down! Restrain them!"

I was to find out later that this Razor's leader's name was Kemp; held true by his mates as a fighter; a champion. He had risen to supreme by fucking and killing the most people, in violent rituals. He was quite young, but he could instil fear into anyone around him. He is psychopathic and that's what helped him rise quickly. Not many would look him in the eye, let alone challenge him and that's the way he liked it.

I remember the first time he looked at me. Chills electrified my whole body as if I knew I were bound for a life of pain at his pleasure. He called me forth, forcefully. "Ario, Transit! Bring her to me!" I held on to my mother's hand in disbelief but was pulled from her by two powerful men. In the dust, I was forced to my knees. "Get the rod." I watched, perplexed, as in front of me, Kemp melted a gold rod down and formed a circular ring with it, which he then moulded into the skin of my neck under my bedraggled mess of brunette hair. Writhing, I screamed in agony as the heat scorched my innocent body. Then I passed out. Only momentarily, as I was forced awake by water thrown over me. My mother and father had been restrained by further men as they tried to get to me.

"No," my father pleaded, "let Alicia go. Take me instead."

Kemp replied scoffingly, "You are nothing to me. Shut up! Your time will come." He then had Smith forge a chain so that he could lead me around like a dog. He renamed me Odalisque, Oda for short. So very different from my birth name, all of which seemed like so long ago. I found out later that I was the only pet that he had ever done this with. It wasn't long before my linen pants had been removed, much to my dismay, and they were replaced by a chastity belt made of scraps of thick tin and metals fastened with a lock – rounded edges, still sharp so that they would cut into me when I moved – for I had not yet come of age. It was an opposing moral to Kemp's normality when in every aspect of his life he didn't seem to carry on any of the old-world societal rulings. I was sacred to him for reasons I didn't know yet. Kemp held the key around his broad neck. I had tried many times to steal it only to end up with him laughing in my face and lending to times of demoralisation. At least one thing was for sure because I belonged to him, no one else touched me; which ironically made me feel safe.

To say the least, being that close to Kemp gave me enough intel to know how to survive in this world we now call Pandemonium. The place itself is like something out of a war zone. From what I was aware of the cities were all but destroyed, playing host to a dictatorship by the Theodoris. The smaller towns in our zone were mostly abandoned; making them home to the local wildlife: spiders, possums and gliders ran wild; nature was ruling, and flora was vast. Leeching vines, listless eucalypts and plumed ferns strangled what was left of the skeletal society of the past. Avoided by most Razor camps.

The encampments were usually set up in vantage points within dense immense and ostrich ferny undergrowth, sumptuously gilt canopies and gigantic wild eucalypt trees. We never knew where we were heading next and wherever we went we didn't stay long for fear of Theodoris invasion. Kemp's protégés were constantly starting new Razor colonies in order to strengthen his own. They were unsettling psychopaths much like him; he always knew how to choose the best of them, and you would hear of them for years to come. But never one to rival Kemp; he was the top dog and had the scars all over his muscularly lean body to prove it. I've seen every inch of his body and if he wasn't such a murderous soul, I'd almost feel sorry for him.

I remember a challenge one day whereby Peter – one of Kemp's protégés tried to take over the camp. Kemp laughed as Peter strained to battle him in the scrub. "You haven't got it in you, Peter." He toyed.

"You're outdated, Kemp. I'll skin you like a pig when I'm finished with you." It was quite obvious that Peter was not ready, but it was amusement for Kemp, and they hadn't raided a camp for a few days at least. Peter was a strong left-handed man who always led with a right jab, which was a weakness. Certainly, Kemp had worked this out quite early as Peter was covered in blood from the knife attacks to his side. Kemp, although wounded, looked more like a kid in a candy store; playing with this teenager. The roar of the crowd rang out, and the entire time I could not help but admire Kemp's calmness. It was almost methodical. In fact, he was methodical in everything he did; except when it came to me. Really it was dependent upon what mood he was in. Kemp switched from spirited to a psychopath in a single second and when that happened Peter's fate was sealed. "You're fucked now, Peter! Banishment. Smith, brand him."

The branding tool was made from a steel piece forged by Smith and had the symbol of an acute triangle to show that they were less than worthy which meant that most of these outcasts, if not killed within the week because of the weight it held, became a sub-clan who would go about their own ventures – avoiding Kemp and his scouts all together. For once branded it was not only a death wish from Kemp but all other Razor tribes as well, as he was the driving force for them all.

Chapter 2

As soon as I came of age – that was it for me. I became his sex slave as well as his trophy. He hardly ever let me out of his sight. Kemp's curiosity had turned into an obsession and there was no way to refuse him as he would always have something or someone to use against me if I didn't do exactly what he had asked; my brother being one of them.

It was my brother that I first witnessed, seeming centuries ago, to turn. He used to be strong-willed yet adventurously quiet. We used to run wildly through the eucalypt forests and climb the sheer horridly black and belittling cliff sides of the mountains that encapsulated our settlement. Looking for anything to spark our creativity and playfulness. We would find grassy fields and enthusiastically look up at the pleasantly intoxicating clouds trying to guess what each of them beheld. Koalas would sit serenely in the ever-present gums and we would pick flowers from the wattle trees and bulbs from the banksias. The large pods of the pea flowers reminded me of a storybook my mother shared with me when I was young by the author May Gibbes, encompassing the gum nut babies. We would use tea tree leaves in teas for comfort and their oils for ailments. The red and purple ochre that lay a crest would become our paints, the smooth and precipitous rocks our pallets and the monstrously ancient cave walls our canvases. Drawing what we could remember of our younger times. Days when the light was all around, and we felt safer. But we would also illustrate the other settlements as reminders that we were not alone. We would imagine who would be the perfect couples in our camps and be pleased with ourselves when our foresight proved true.

Chase was only 10 months older than me; taller, leaner, brunette short hair and blue eyes, eighteen years old. They swooped in on him and in Razor form gave him a knife and a choice; his own life or someone else's. "It's up to you," Kemp threatened, "your knife or mine?"

The nightmares still haunt me of the fear in his eyes and the love in my father's. There was no choice. If he had left it to Kemp, it would have been a slow and painful death but if he completed the ultimate sin then at least it would be quick and relatively painless; for dad at least. I know it still haunts Chase to this day. He is forever scarred and relatively silent because of what had happened, that terrifying unknowable day and the epoch that came.

I watched on with my mother as they strung Dad up from the eerie eucalypt in front of us. Kemp whispered something in my father's ear whilst directly looking at me. It was then my father writhed on the tree, but it was to no avail. My brother was violently shaking as he motioned towards Dad. "I'm sorry, Dad." He kept spouting as he sauntered forward.

"It's OK, son," was Dad's reply.

Kemp began a countdown. "10… 9…" The tribe joined in. "8… 7…" Frightened tears fell from Chase's face, unsteadily he held the knife to Dad's Adam's apple, allowing a bead in the form of a droplet of blood to flow from his throat.

"3… 2…" He steadied his right arm with his left, closed his eyes and, "2… 1…" slit Dad's throat from one end to the other. The blood drained with a naturally quick flow in a bright red hue and he was gone. The screaming started around me, and the hatred was firmly embedded. I eyeballed Kemp and gnarled. I would get my revenge. Chase cried profusely along with my mother, weeping as they took her to the next closest tree. In contrast, a beautiful wattle. Three of them pinned her to the ground, another held Chase and I was then tied to the gum tree with my father's blood flowing over the wounded tree's sap and onto my head. They tore her clothes from her innocent body and one after the other they had their way with her. In violent acts; Kemp was always the first, and then the others followed. They made her do the unthinkable, with the threat of both Chase and I being hung like our father; reaching the same fate. They made us watch, through our protests, every minute of the mutilations and sexualisation of my mother's poor body. Until she could no longer expanse any energy and lay there silent, seemingly numb, traumatised; looking right through us. My mother was no longer there; she was only a shadow of her former self.

I will never forget that moment and I vowed not ever to allow myself to feel again. That is, no other feeling but revenge on this clan of rapists and murderers, or any other Razor that I would come into contact with. I had lost all sense of pacifism and as the blood of my father grew thicker in my hair, my hate grew stronger, my blue eyes defiant. I did not hate my brother for his choice but rather pitied him for what he would have to live with and how he would have to live now; once a Razor, always a Razor, or so I thought.

In order to further implant Chase's killer psychological state, he was then subjected to ritualised torture for countless days. In his better nature, Chase tried to defy the laws imposed upon him, but this only added more scarring to his body and his mind. He was slowly losing his psyche to the environment's schizophrenic nature. Soon enough the paranoia swelled from inside and my once playful brother was no more than the character of a Razor, even though I only saw hollowness in his eyes. Under the close watch of his superior Caelin, he continued his training. He was no longer Chase but a Razor at heart.

My fate I was still unsure of, but the chains strewed from my neck I hoped, like all other things in this world, would not last forever. I was hesitant about how this would unravel but like all worldly things, I prayed it would come to an end, once driven its course. At first, I was kept in Kemp's cage in his tent. His bed was made of hay and wood, a firepit lay lazily in the corner. Beside the bed was a wooden cup and an almost empty glass wine bottle on a wooden table. There were other things in the room, but I didn't understand what they could be, until later when I was hung or bound to each apparatus. The cage I was to call my home was made of iron, but the lock was fickle; hay lay on the grassy floor and a bowl in the corner. Confinement did not come naturally to me so in the beginning I fought contentiously with all of my might and a few times I was able to escape, but only to be caught by his militia at the entrance to the tent and chastised. The lock was re-evaluated and tightened. I was allowed out at certain times for hygiene reasons, always with two guards, but mostly to be showcased as a trophy to other Razor clan leaders, or to be used to coerce my brother into continuing his training.

The camp was organised, all around the pivotal fire. Razors were busy working; cooking, sharpening blades, reassembling bows, making bullets and the like. There were lots of small tents made of calico, they used larger branches as the posts and poles to hold the tents together. The shelters were assembled in a circle with the cooking fire in the middle along with any supplies. Tall tumultuous trees swayed in the wind, towering over the primitive tents and a delicate plethora of ferns filled the undergrowth. It was a secure setup.

The wounds on my brothers and my skin would never heal and were a constant reminder of the brutality of man but it wasn't that which I was concerned about; it was the slashing of our hearts and the misplacing of our minds that troubled me. My mother used to say to us, "Kindness and love will keep you safe." But this as I have learnt is only in part truth. She was still alive and still a plaything in the hands of Kemp's militia but existed only as a shell. A defence of her own. My father, in Razor style, was carved up, cooked in front of us and fed to us piece by piece over a matter of weeks. I would vomit every time I was forced to eat a piece of him, but they would make me eat that too until there was nothing left. Even his bones were ground into meals and used to supplement our diet. But this regime was the fuel for my revenge. I would have to, through gritted teeth, succumb to authoritarianism just to survive.

I came of age too soon. I was eighteen when my reality was distorted, and my sexual innocence was stolen. I don't know how many women Kemp had slept with before then but that first night I was petrified; for I'd only seen what other Razors had done to captive women as well as what Kemp had done to them out in the open. They would be ripped from one end to the other, as some of the torture techniques were highly medieval and outright cruel. A variation of the Judas cradle was used, the screaming victim lowered onto the point of a triangle, piercing their spine leaving them paralysed as a great number of different men, brawled to enter the victim, while their own husbands or wives were forced to watch. But with me he was possessive, keeping me inside of his tent.

I was well developed for an 18-year-old and he was well advanced for 21. Dragging me out of my cage he held me to the floor with one arm – intense eyes staring into mine – and slowly slid the knife across my dress, tearing what had not cut, exposing my body, but he did not take it off. I trembled as he ran the knife over and into my skin seeming to relish every moment of it, blood dripping from my thin arms. Kemp turned me over and I felt the knife carve something into my back. A name? A branding? I did not know. I winced at the pain of it, but I remembered it clearly, though my vision was blurry, for being beaten. I saw a smeared puddle of velvet-red blood. It was mine, but I felt apart from it. Light-headedness filled my mind and a frozen fear encapsulated my body. All I knew is that I was panicking with what was to come; all the while holding in the screams so as to show no weakness.

I felt the cold steel move further down tracing my abdomen and inner thigh, then a clink as for the first time my chastity belt was released the healing scabs torn as the metal edges scraped my skin. At this point I somehow jolted alive, no longer frozen I began to fight him, to try and push him away from me but it was of no use, it only amused him more. His eyes fixated on me and his muscular arms held me tight. He lowered a barbed wire cage that hung from the highest point of the tent and entrapped my upper body under it. The spikes dug into me; pearls of blood escaped as it tore at my skin. I was imprisoned, naked and vulnerable. Methodically, he took his knife and allowed it to caress my skin from my buttocks through to my toes. Not enough to pierce, but to inspire fear. He began to kiss me in places only I had touched, playfully licking as he went and when he tickled me, I would writhe, and sharp pains would remind me of the spikes embedded in my back.

Sensing my terror, and recognizing he had control, the cage was lifted and by my wrists he pulled me over to the bed, then grazing his hand around my throat he pushed me backwards, the softness of the bed feeling both foreign and unsettling. Leaning against me he slowly took his shirt off; just so I could feel every brush against my cheek as he moved his bare well-built chest was at the height of my face and I could see the small blonde hairs that covered his shoulders. He knelt down and with a patronising smile beckoned me to kiss his thin, pink lips. I struggled in vain as the knife at my throat grew deeper. I kissed him back – only to find him pulling away, playing games, toying with me. Annoyance and confusion filled my mind as he rolled me over forcing my face into the woven blanket, I struggled to free my head unable to breathe. Grasping a chunk of hair in his hands he pushed the back of my head further down, I scratched at his hands as the pounding in my head gave way to light-headedness, I assumed you only experience moments before you die. "You will do as you are told, move only as I order you to, breathe when I let you." Then turning my head to face him, I opened my mouth, taking in as much oxygen as possible. Through the tears in my eyes, I saw him smirk then he released my hair, and brought his hand with force into my face, my body rolling over with the power of his punch. My breasts scratched from the cage were dripping blood slowly and my large cold nipples were rigid, I tried to struggle free, but he proved too strong for me. He took some silk ties from a nearby cabinet. Raising my arms above my head binding my wrists to each corner at the top of the bed, then spreading my legs, he tied my ankles to the two wooden posts that held up the lower end. Grabbing a handful of hay while there he forced the dry twigs into my mouth. The last silk he wrapped around the handle of the knife and left a few inches dangling from the bottom of it. I felt completely exposed.

Heat moved to my face as beads of panicked sweat skimmed my nose falling to my upper lip. He saw this and moved to where I was red. Using the silk tail from the knife he ran it across my forehead and over my eyes. Again, he pressured me to kiss him, this time pressing his arm across my collarbone. It was a demand and he pushed hard against me until the pain of his weight made me kiss him hard back. Taking his lip between my teeth I bit him, which only turned him on more as he let the blood drip from his lips onto mine. Using his arm against my chest he pushed into me lifting his torso off my body, the pain so sharp, I thought any moment now my collarbone would be snapped in two. His arm finally left my chest, and too soon he was standing over me his feet on either side of my thighs. Undoing the leather strap, he used as a belt, then raising his arm in the air, down came the strap against my rib cage over and over, the marks had made my stomach slippery with blood. My screams went unanswered.

Using the knife, he ripped what little was left of my dress from me and threw it wildly against the wall, leaving it blood-stained and sullen on the floor. I had frozen again. The fear of it all had penetrated my mind and stopped me from all movement and he could sense it, like an eagle to its prey. He placed the knife on my chest and slowly unravelled the silk from it so that I could feel the sensations of steel and silk across my skin until it bubbled with goosebumps. I squirmed under it and as my blood started pumping again my fight kicked in, little did I know this was just what he wanted.

Undoing the silk scarves, he pinned my elbows to the table and violently sucked on my neck. I could feel the blood rising and my arms were already bruising. Slowly but aggressively, he moved his way down to my chest, all the while I could feel his eyes searching for mine, but I dared not look. He grabbed me by my hair, his bicep bulging as it pulled, he was trying to make me gaze at him, but I closed my eyes shutting them tight. He began to bite at my neck and the pain was almost unbearable, but I wasn't going to let him see me hurting, he was enjoying this.

As he moved further down, one hand dragged my head forward and the other pulled my right buttock up, out and towards him. He was still wearing pants, but I could feel him getting harder against my groin, which made me open my eyes in fear. He took his hand and slowly licked his fingers, and then with one swift movement he pulled down on my shoulder, bit my neck and penetrated me behind. I squealed as he moved further inside my backside pushing hard and fast; the pain only slightly subsided by the biting on my neck and the reefing on my shoulder. I felt so degraded. Anger, fear and tears rolled into one as I tried to lean back but his strength was too much for me. He had me, and that's the way he wanted it, so that's the way it would be. Turning me over he grew firmer against my groin moving his mouth slowly across my face and lips, down my neck to my breasts. Smiling sadistically.

Clamping my inner leg as if to strangle, I could almost feel the future bruising. Then using both hands, pulling me close at the waist, he started to circulate my left breast with his tongue. I couldn't stop it from betraying me, standing on end as he got closer to the nipple, licking delicately which seemed strange after the vicious attack on the rest of my body. Guilt consumed me. He moved to the right breast, mimicking the other, its nipple stood on end; all the while he grew firmer between my legs. I could feel myself getting wet below and the more I tried to stop it, the worse it got. Then he stopped. Left the room. And left me there. Naked. Alone. Violated. Confused. It was very un-Kemp actually. Being so systematic he usually made sure that he finished what he started but for some reason, he just left. Sitting, I curled into a ball on the bed. Lost.

It wasn't long before he came back in with a bunch of miscellaneous items; amongst them, candles, rope and two other guys. Another abnormality – but I soon became aware of why two of his trusted militia were there. They tied my feet together with rope and made me kneel before Kemp. One of them lit the candle and started dripping wax on my shoulders; slowly at first, and then at a much more rapid pace all the while the other held me in place. They were too strong for me to break loose but at least I still had my hands to attempt to push them away. The candle wax burnt my skin and the honeycomb got caught in the cuts made by the knife. They taunted me with a whip and took pleasure in choking me slowly with a silk scarf almost to the point of passing out.

Kemp watched on, seated, legs spread wide and with a twisted smile.

I tried not to scream but my yelps were heard from nearby tents, mocking and laughter were the responses that came from within them. Kemp observed me like some kind of animal while Transit the first militant, a nuggety-looking fellow, pulled the silk firmly around my eyes blind folding me – cutting off all sight. It was at this point that my heart was beating so fast that I thought I was going to die. They beat me, whipped me, waxed me, tied my hands together behind my back and held me so tight that even though I struggled I could not move.

Strangely, it suddenly all stopped, and a soft gentle breath brushed past my ear. I was now aware that Kemp was near. I could smell the excitement coming from his innermost being. Footsteps left the room and I knew that I was alone with him again. He leaned towards me and whispered in my ear. "Now be a good girl and do exactly as I say, or I will send Chase to the front line and murder him myself. He will suffer a slow and painful death." I shuddered, and in my mind, I was besieged, not knowing what to do and what would be done to me.

I whispered back tentatively, "Anything you want." And with this Kemp pushed against me, submitting I made my way to the floor and he told me to stay there. I was in a prone position. I was exposed.

Kemp soundlessly moved behind me and lightly licked my backside, until making his way towards the middle again. This time he didn't penetrate with his fingers but rather playfully rotated his tongue like a whirlpool, and just as quickly he pulled me in by my hips and then grabbed my breasts with fierce animosity. Without my hands, I had only my chin to keep me balanced. He moved slightly lower to a part that had never been touched before and as much as I felt violated, I was guilty enough to admit that it felt good too. He thrashed with me, pulling in my hips with one strong muscular arm towards him, licking my vulva and inside of my vagina all while spiritedly playing with his penis until it was as hard as a rock. Apart from Kemp's mild groans everything was silent. That was until he started licking further up towards the top of my swollen vulva and under the fire-coloured polar hood that protected my powerfully sensitive clitoris. A sensation of excitement fled through my body and I tried to resist with all of my might but with the pulling, pushing, licking, sucking, and the inevitability of my wetness I couldn't help but cry with pleasure; against my better nature.

He then stopped pleasuring himself and moved his hand to harden my breasts all while rocking my body with his elbows and stroking my clitoris with his tongue. My chin was hurting as it pushed up against the matted hay and my vagina tightened with the realisation that this could be happening soon. I was frightened and tensed my whole body. Kemp responded straight away. He undid my leg ties, pulled back my hair and my hips, laid me down and penetrated me so deeply that all I could do was scream in agony while he fucked and fucked me.

It seemed like hours before he stopped and moved me to the bed tying me to one of the cornices, uncovered my eyes and tied my mouth with the silk. His tight lips were pursed, and I could see it in his eyes that he was not yet satisfied. A smirk drifted across his face and fear fleeted across mine. I had known him for months now and this was a definite gnarled look of deviancy. The kind he has when he knows he has ultimate control. At this point, I knew I was his slave. Nothing I could do would prevent that nor prolong what was to happen next.

Startling me, he slapped me hard across the face and his whole demeanour changed. His eyes glazed over, and he was no longer Kemp but a demon. He took me and through my protests, he continued to fuck me hard, until I could no longer fight or move. There was no decency or respect left in me. I felt hollow and most of all everywhere hurt. I don't just mean my physical self but my emotional self as well. He left me lying there naked and bloody. He just left. Again. Outside I could hear cheers and laughter as the Razors worshipped him and his dominance over me. But this was not the worst of it, nor the end; it was only the beginning of what was to become my living nightmare.

Within the hour my brother was sent in to lock the chastity belt back on and to put me back into my cage. Not a word was spoken between us but from his eyes, I concluded that he too was thinking about how to seek revenge, for deep down in his psyche I knew that he still loved me. It had been ingrained in us from our childhood. Before locking me away he put me in a nearby bath and took a washer and some aloe and began to wipe away the blood stains on my body and to pad up where I had lost my virginity in order to clean where the flow of blood was. I cried profusely now, and all we could see was red and in both of us, I could feel a mutual bond. We both played our parts but deep down we knew that this was and is still not us; nor will it be the end. I smiled at him sincerely and he managed a smirk back but then he was taken from me, it was the last glance I saw of him for a while. I will never forget those watery, glazed eyes of his and no matter what they did to Chase I will never forget the memories of our childhood; the only thing keeping me sane at this point.

For nights on end Kemp would visit me; ritualising our moments together; him dominating, me submitting but it wasn't too long before he got more and more violent with me. It was almost as if he needed to take all of his frustrations out on someone and the fights and raids on Settlers weren't doing it for him anymore. The more girls he was with the more insatiable his thirst was for me and my blood.

When walking in one night, Kemp had a sadistic glare in his eyes – he had raided nearby camps just moments before and didn't bother to prepare me. Instead, he undressed on his way in and after dragging me from the cage, he hit me so hard I stumbled and struggled to see. I felt like I was speeding through a dark passage filled with sounds of laughter and roaring. My eyes were too tired to open, and I couldn't really see properly or be mentally coherent enough to be able to piece anything together quite yet anyway. Eventually, consciousness set in and a ringing in my ears began to bug me and to top it off I had an excruciatingly, agonizing headache. I realised at that moment that the firm chastity belt fixed around my waist was gone and I was left lying naked in a pool of what looked like my own blood. It was getting worse. It was like he didn't want me to remember any of it, but I did remember. I would awake at night after dreaming of the horrific things that he had done to me and it was then that I knew that they would never leave, that he was ingrained in me.

I had seen Kemp with other women before and I knew how cruel and violent he was, but I couldn't understand for the life of me what had happened to create this change. What had I done wrong? I had done everything he had asked of me and yet he continued to get worse. It must have had something to do with the knock on the head that had cut my short-term memory because as I went to rise, I found myself chained from all fours and it was then it dawned on me what had happened. If it wasn't for the throbbing pain in my head, I may have noticed the other areas that had been mutilated but all I could do at that time was fall onto the table and lay in unconsciousness. At least – excluding the nightmares – I felt safe there.

He didn't send my brother in this time. Instead, he sent two of his men to wash me clean. They weren't as delicate, nor did they care about what they did or didn't do to me. I was still in a state of non-clarity and the incoherence made me not care anyway. They could do to me what they willed as long as I could be put back into my cage to once again be safe from these attacks.

This was going on for months now and perhaps Kemp was getting aggravated with me, so I started to think of ways to seduce him; only to make it less painful for me. So instead of fighting him, I started to use my sexual prowess to make him feel more powerful, to show him that I felt sexually attracted to him and liked the way he dominated me. I played on his ego, his masculinity. I started to make attractive noises which made him want to fuck me harder. I would whisper in his ear seductively, telling him how much I enjoyed his power over me. Telling him that I wanted him all the time; that I could not live without him and then I would guide him to my breasts and my thighs until he would get so firm that, at times, we were actually fucking almost like a normal couple. Of course, he could not give up his dominance and possession, but I made sure that the campsite knew that he was good at what he did, even if I was faking it.

This reflected well on my brother who rose in the ranks, quickly becoming a sniper and in command of some troops, so it was working out OK for both of us. I was still not allowed out of my cage and still wore my belt, but Kemp would come and visit me on more than one occasion throughout the day softening as the months went by. He would still put me into vulnerable positions, bent over whatever he could find, and when he had had a hard day, I would know about it. He would become violent again and I would need more aloe and bathing but at least I had a handmaiden now to help with all of this.

Her name was Sabe and she was found in one of the settlements north of where we had set up camp at the time. A few years older than me she had been tortured and raped but was now protected as my guardian, with one male to keep her in check. She would tend to my wounds; make sure that I was healthy; she knew about all of the natural remedies and bush foods of the area. This is where I learnt most of my healing techniques and all about foods that were poisonous and foods that were useful for a variety of different needs. In particular, those plants and foods with anti-inflammatory properties and those that aided in the stopping of blood loss and healing of scars.

Chapter 3

Life continued in camp as usual and as months went by, we moved again, this time to a place they called Blood Stone. Many battles had been fought there but it was a safe enough place as the Theodoris in particular were too superstitious to go to this sacred place. On one of my walks, I could see the camp. Blood Stone definitely had an eerie feel about it. The wind whistled through the trees making them almost lyrical in their actions. There were a lot of people in this camp and I would imagine even more scouts hidden from view. The mountains towered above us and there was what I supposed was a stream nearby, noted by the trickling sounds almost drowned out by the Razor's chatter.

The first night Kemp came to me with what looked like a pacifier, except it covered my teeth and he told me to put it on. Confused, I did what he asked, and I used my seductive eyes to try and calm him so that he would not be so forceful with me. Sometimes this worked but tonight he had an agenda. He brought Sabe in with one of the militants, her man, they called him Ario. Ario was shorter than Kemp, a lean man with dense brown eyes. He bathed me every now and then, in fact, he did whatever Kemp wanted, wherever he wanted. Kemp's most trusted man. Ario held Sabe close to him and the scene was unusual because it had been a while since Kemp and I were accompanied by someone else. Kemp undressed me and turned me so that my back was against his chest and made me watch as Ario started to undress Sabe. Slowly but under duress, she participated until naked before him. The knife held to her throat was a dead giveaway that something wasn't right there. Ario told Sabe to get on her knees and take off his pants. Sabe looked at me knowingly as if in unspoken words to say, it's OK. I struggled to get to her, but Kemp had me pinned tightly to his chest. "Now watch," he whispered in my ear.

Not knowing what to think, I gazed on as Sabe was forced to have oral sex with Ario. Whenever she did something he disliked, he would whip her and hold the knife to her throat in force. She too had a mouthpiece and I watched on in shock as she slowly made his cock bulge with ferocity. I could feel Kemp push against me, and he whispered again, "Make sure you take note of everything." I shuddered at the thought that Kemp now wanted me to do this with him. That he trusted me even? I was sure to bite his penis off well before putting it anywhere near my mouth. But I did take note, I watched as she circled the top of his penis, where she put her hands, how she used her tongue and what made him both happy and mad at her. In a place like this, you needed to learn quickly. I was just hoping that it was not going to be me doing this tonight.

Ario started groaning as Sabe got deeper and deeper onto his penis until finally he pushed her forcefully onto the bed and fucked her until he was satisfied. I was shocked and both Sabe and Ario got dressed leaving the room as silently as they came in.

It was just Kemp and me, I was shaking, and Kemp could feel the contention inside of me. I knew him and if I was not perfect, then I would be in for the night of my life. He tied me above the bed with my arms secured against the wooden pole that hung above me and he got a candle from inside of his black box. Lighting it, he layered the wax over my collar bones, melting it towards my breasts. He had my nipples covered just enough so that they would stand on end as the warmth moved towards them. He then robustly clamped them into place so that my breasts were paralysed with both pain and pleasure. I had definitely gotten used to it and it turned me on so much that I would immediately start to get wet below, but he wouldn't touch me, just drive me crazy with his antics, to keep in control. He lowered me to my knees and standing firmly on the bed beside me began to undress; both hastily and untidily. It was then that I realised that he wanted me to fuck him orally. Did he trust me that much? I was more than likely going to make his life a living hell if he even put that thing near my mouth but it's not like I had much choice.

As I tensed, he noticed the change and began to caress my body with the tips of his fingers. I realised then that he was taller than most men. The wax brought me back, it still lingered around my breasts, but the rest of my body tingled in protest and I started to pulse. Unlike before he started kissing me gently behind my ears, sucking on my lobes and swirling around my neck. The groans came naturally this time and I barely had time to notice that I was actually enjoying this. I needed to take my head to another space as my body deceived me. He lingered, smelling my hair and breathing along my wet neck. He leaned in to kiss me and I couldn't help but want him back. But playfully, he got in close beckoning me and stopping before I could respond. I wanted him. I didn't want him. Disillusionment engulfed me as he leaned back and then confusion encroached upon me as he put his spell on me. To my astonishment, he was seducing me. Had he worked me out? Was my secret of toying with him out as well?

Lowering me even further he laid me on my back and in one swoop pulled me in and began kissing me from abdomen to groin. My nipples hardened further, and I was completely under his hex. He manoeuvred between kissing, licking me and biting which made me even more encapsulated but I was still consumed with thoughts of his ulterior motives. He moved further down, making me quiver more as he pushed at my hips, spreading my thighs and continuing down my groin to my toes. Pulsing, I felt challenged and kicked to snap myself out of it, but it only made him more committed to his motivations. I caught a glimpse of his green eyes looking up at me as he slowly worked his way back up to where the pulsing had begun. Breathing gently, he teased me, and everything slowed. He would not touch me but rather reefed me back into a kneeling position. I could now see his penis erect and vivacious. This was it. I had to perform now, but what do I do? I tried to remember back to Sabe and what she had done but my mind went completely blank with paralysis. It was all up to me now. He undid the ropes that bound my hands above my head; his first sign of trust but not yet vulnerability. He slowly pulled my head back and very carefully I looked into his eyes. He was insatiable.

He drew my head in towards the foreskin of his penis and guided me to suck and lick gently under and around the head. I could tell he was uneasy for the first time ever. But for me, now was the time to gain his trust. I found the lip on the glands on the knob of his penis and rolled my tongue gently around it whilst sucking on his tip. Weirdly, it enlarged further as the foreskin pulled back and I could feel him trembling with this new exposure. Using my hands, I grabbed his buttocks, taking a leaf from his book and cupped him from behind. His groaning increased with every pull, so I started to push him further in, making sure that I caressed the most sensitive parts. By this point, he went wild and started thrusting causing me to begin to choke, so using one of my hands I grabbed and worked the shaft of his penis and vehemently embraced him making him grunt with excitement. But it wasn't enough for him. He continued to force me, pushing my head further along his shaft until I had him firmly in my throat, pulsing violently. I moved my tongue right under the ridge of Kemp's penis and while moving his foreskin forward and back he let go of my head and in one last groan orgasmed right before my eyes. I took it all in, so as not to aggravate him.

I could finally remove the piece from my mouth as he lay there, not even concerned that I was free to do whatever I liked. In any case I was too scared to move just in case one of his henchmen caught me and did something worse. As Kemp lay there, I had a million thoughts going through my mind. What do I do now? It wasn't long before the choice was made for me.

The alert was sounded, and Kemp jumped up, grabbed me by the arm and threw me back in my cage. He was running to command, he met at the tent door with Barrett – his second in charge. The Theodoris had found our camp and every Razor stood to attention, fully armed and ready for their engagement. "They never come here," Barrett exclaimed. "Why now?" But that wasn't a matter of concern for Kemp;

he was already in the process of ordering his Razors into defensive positions and the archers and snipers into attack mode. I could hear the yells as he stationed them everywhere, and I couldn't help but admire his methodology. We had been invaded before but never by an encroaching Theodoris squadron. It was just lucky that they had not yet noticed what they had walked into. From what I could see through the gaping hole in the tent, a lot of the squad would have been wiped out by snipers and archers before they could even set foot on base. The others were now in full-scale combat in the quadrant. We were at a disadvantage in one aspect as they were armed to the hilt but in other respects, it looked like more of a scout group, so it wasn't long before Kemp had taken control of the situation and the few hostages left were on their knees ready for interrogation.

"Where is your base camp?" Kemp was yelling furiously.

But there was no response from the Theodoris. They had been trained well. I knew this was going to be a torturous morning as one of the men was pulled from the pack and hung from his arms in front of the others. Smith brought out the branding tools and Barrett the torture devices; mainly knives and scalpels. One way or another they were going to get it out of them. The women that were left were taken behind the hanging invader and Kemp's people began their torture on them as well. It had been a while since an invasion, so they were insatiably violent with them. They saw it as their right, to take them as their own possessions.

Kemp bellowed again, "Where the fuck is your base camp?"

Knowing full well that the base was now in danger because a scout would have been sent back to alert any others, the rest of the camp was in full swing, packing up and getting ready to move out. It was still strange that the Theodoristes had come to this God-forsaken place. They must have been getting bolder, or losing more ground, or more likely we had a rat in our midst.

Chase was sent to lead the ground sweep taking the Razors out of the camp to search for tracks and to try and find the scouts before they made it back to their base. So, I could only hope for his sake that it hadn't been set up as a trap.

With no response from the Theodoris, Kemp beckoned to Barrett to begin the ritual. First, they drugged him with a bush plant called Hyoscine; it was a truth serum, and then they slit him from throat to navel, taking off his clothes to reveal his nakedness. The blood flow was just enough to keep him alive and to let the serum take over. Watching on, the other soldiers who had obviously been trained well – stayed calm and seemingly rational throughout. But this man could not resist the serum and within moments Kemp had all of the information he needed.

The Theodoris site was mobile and based but a few kilometres from where we were camped. So, another scout was sent by horse to catch the others on foot and scope out their site. Why they were here? A tipoff from a Razor amidst our camp had got to Peter and had sent them to find us in order to kill off every last one of us. It would be the only chance for the Theodoris to take over if they could kill Kemp. The Theodoris at the camp were beheaded and left hanging by their ankles as a warning.

At once Kemp sent a squad to look for another site and set up a group of his finest warriors to be deployed to destroy the other Theodoris site. Kemp got Ario and Sabe to look after me and we were on the move east towards the rainforest. Ario was put in charge of finding a suitable site and the rest of the Razors followed his orders from then on in. I was put back into chains and tied to Ario and we moved at a quick pace. It was difficult to walk in chains and I found myself stumbling through the forest's tumultuous floor. But it wasn't long before we found a place that was confined between a large arrangement of humped boulders, and the Razors set up camp there, where I was put back in my cage.

It wasn't until a few days later we heard the call from the deployed and with luck, I saw Chase again, bloodied and bruised, but still alive. Kemp, as per usual, with his extraordinary fighting skills was able to remain unscathed, but his temper was elevated. There were no survivors from the Theodoris camp, and they did not bother with the ritualistic keeping of the bodies for meat but rather left them there to rot as a sign to any others that would dare come close to our Razor camp.

Instead of taking it out on me, he first rallied the Razors, knowing full well that there was a traitor in our midst. The mob stood silently as Kemp screamed abuse calling forward the deserter. But it was to no avail, of course, no one was going to own up. So, Kemp got the apothecary Benedict, a weedy-looking guy, to develop a mass amount of hyoscine in the hope of getting the truth out of the rest of the people at our new base. It wasn't long before Rachel who had heard one of the others talking about the raid said that Jaakobah was the one who spilled. The problem was that he was lost in all of the rigmarole along with a few of the other Razors. She also mentioned something about Peter who was siding with the Theodoris and had been trying to take out Razor camps for weeks now. Kemp was ropable, and Rachel's fate was sealed. She was now to become a pet.

Kemp, Ario, Caelin, Transit, and a few other trusted militants gathered in my tent and it was only in brutal imaginations what they were plotting. A group of scouts were sent out to contact the other camps to meet somewhere safe in order to begin to band together and kill off Peter's cluster. The only problem was that according to Rachel his group had grown in size immensely, so Kemp would need a lot more of the Razors to come on board in order to combat this resistance. Also, with the Theodoris alliance, they would need to do a lot of scouting and downsize our own camp supplies to become more mobile, so as not to get caught off guard.

It wasn't long before everything was in full swing and through the tent, I could see all sorts of movement. Mobile traps were being set, Razors were upping their skills, and everyone was on high alert. Within a couple of days, scouts and their leaders had come from everywhere and plans for full-scale warfare were being put into place. At least at this point, Kemp was busy elsewhere which gave me a chance to recover as I watched on.

Chapter 4

I didn't know the details of what was to happen, but I knew the raids were getting closer when Kemp came for me again. This time he was not alone. It seemed like he wanted more than just me this time. He bought in a girl that they had captured, dark olive skin, long blonde hair and a slim build, and within seconds he had roped her to the hanging bar above the table. He pulled me from my cage and bound me to his ankle using a chain and brace. I'm guessing this was to give me just enough freedom to do what he wanted but not enough to get away. The woman looked older but who knew these days? It didn't take a rocket scientist to work out what he wanted though. It was just how this was going to play out that really disillusioned me. And I couldn't pick his mood. He seemed calm but wanted a performance. Luckily, he was a control freak, so he provided most of the instruction and the rest I had learnt from him working me over. He motioned for me to go to the girl and he whispered in my ear, "I want you to seduce her."

'Shit' was all I could think. I knew that if I didn't Kemp would get rough with her and treat her like one of the Razor pets, so I had to think quickly. How do I gain her trust? And how do I get her to want to be with me? Especially considering I have never been with a woman and I'm guessing by the fear on her face she hadn't either – let alone had any idea as to what was going on. I whispered back to Kemp, "You need to trust me if you want this to happen." He nodded tentatively and called for Ario to stand guard.

I slowly walked towards her and asked if I could lower her from the bar and she agreed. I could feel Kemp cringing behind me. I let her down just enough so that she had the freedom to sit down. She was trembling. "You will need to be strong," I said to her. "And you will need to let me do what I want. If I ask you to do something, you will need to do that too. Otherwise, they will send you to the Razor guards out there and they are not who you want to be with right now. OK?" She nodded, and I knew that at this point she was ready to conform.

"You are so beautiful." I explored. "In fact, I know that we are going to get along just fine."

I looked into her brown eyes and tentatively asked, "What's your name?"

"Rose."

She began to relax which made me relax more as I knew what would happen to both of us if she did not concede. I moved in behind her and began to lightly massage her shoulders and upper back then lightly rubbing my fingers along her neck I began to kiss her gently from behind – starting from her ears and moving gently to her neck. I could feel her shiver, but she was still tense and unsure. Kemp watched intently, and I made sure that I made eye contact with him continuously in order to keep him stable. I put my thumbs on her bare neck and rested my fingers on her shoulders moving gently down her collarbones. I could tell that she had been with someone before as she responded almost immediately with tremors of comfort throughout her body. I added a little more pressure for Kemp's sake, and she took a deep breath in. Slowly and intently, I began gently kissing her shoulders and massaging lower down her back. I could tell Kemp was getting annoyed at the gentleness of it all, so I moved to the front of her and he tugged me by the chain, so he could see what I was doing.

I gently grazed my lips over hers, teasing her and teasing Kemp. I could tell he was starting to ease. I pulled her hair gently back exposing her neck and started to softly bite, lick and kiss as I went. With my other hand, I slowly undressed her, just the top, and exposed her supple nipples so that Kemp could see them. I moved my hands around her collarbone and teased her with light kisses to her mouth. She was no amateur. But I didn't allow us to kiss fully yet. I moved my hands to the outside of her breasts and started kissing her chest and the outside of her breasts, brushing lightly on her nipples to make them stand on end. She touched me back caressing the small of my back, trying to pull me in, but I would not let her. Moving upward, I flippantly ran my tongue over her bottom lip. Kemp began to masturbate. We could see him lightly stroking himself, but not enough for a full erection. I knew then it was time for me to harden my kiss on her.

I caressed her nipples as I gently played with her lips. Soon enough I had her hair pulled back and we were kissing passionately. It was then I undid the rope and pulled her dress over her head. Kemp flinched but with Ario there, I knew she couldn't or wouldn't dare try to get away. I laid her on the bed and touched the small of her back and in between her thighs. She was breathing heavily now. Her nipples were standing on end and I could sense the wetness between her thighs. I continued to compliment her on how beautiful she was; her body, her demeanour, anything to keep her with me and out of the violent hands of the other Razors. I began kissing her abdomen and that's when Kemp snuck up behind me. Just as I was licking the inside of her thighs, he shelved my head back and told me to stay in that position. As he kissed my neck seductively, he massaged the inside of Rose's thighs, she shuddered but knew better than to move. He whispered in my ear, "You're mine." As if I didn't know that already, but I continued with the power play. Grabbing me around the waist, he lifted my dress over my head and moved his hands across my breasts. "Now tie her to the cornice." He commanded me while undressing himself.

I took her ankle and tied her in. Kemp tied me to the other one and began working me over. He wasn't gentle but violent in his actions – showing off to Rose – trying to make her scared so that she would do whatever he asked. He held his knife to my throat and threatened me not to make a move. Then he made me watch as he went down on Rose – she kept her eyes on me and like me her body betrayed her, she began to groan. Kemp then pulled me in, commanding me to go down on her. He lay underneath me and started stroking my breasts and licking my clitoris. I could feel Rose getting wetter and beginning to shake, she was moaning and as she grew louder Kemp moved in behind me and began fucking me from behind. I could feel myself losing concentration as he penetrated me deeply but continued to play in order to make Rose cum. It wasn't long before both Rose and Kemp were moaning together and in one accord they came together.

Kemp slumped over me and Rose lay still. Ario was there in a moment, dressed her and took her away.

Kemp changed his tune then, he was pissed! He put me into a strappado position with my legs sectioned apart with a spreader; he covered my mouth with a tape gag and looked at me callously. Kemp then asked Ario to come in with a battery and two cables, a pin and some clamps. He was definitely in a mood and this was all new to me. Kemp started calling me names, much like those of the victims he took, "You're nothing but a stupid whore. You're worthless and that's why you can't cum. But don't worry, I'll make you cum, but first, you need to be put back in line." He was no longer the Kemp I knew but the psychopathic Kemp that most knew him by.

He began whipping me, hard, like he needed to get rid of all of his aggression and he was taking it out on me. It hurt so badly that even the gag couldn't stop me from yelling. He kept calling me names and degrading me as he went. He whipped my back, my buttocks, my breasts, and my vagina until all were red with blood and I was struggling to hold myself up by the arms. One thing was for sure, it didn't stop his erection, it only made him stiffer. He was devilish and loved it. He got Ario to put the battery together with the chords and he sparked them together in front of me. I was frozen with fear by this point not knowing at what point he was going to stop. Was he going to kill me?

While Ario was playing with the electricity, Kemp clamped my genitals with pegs and in both shock and fear, I let out a scream. He soon moved to my breasts and this was when I knew that I was in trouble. The peg clamps were made of steel and that electricity being showcased before me was definitely not for display. Kemp beckoned for the chords and with one foul swoop, he attached them to my buttocks making electricity pulse through my body. I couldn't help but scream in agony and before I could scream the second time, Kemp had Ario bring in his henchmen to watch. It was the most humiliating moment of my life. He continued to electrocute me in different places as they watched on with sickening smiles on their faces. Kemp was just showing off now. Each of them unbuttoned their trousers and started masturbating around me, laughing with every yell that I took. Soon the pain turned to nothingness as a fog filled my mind and with each of them coming before my eyes it sickened me even more. How could he do this? Why was he doing this?

They were then all asked to leave, and it was just me and him. But it wasn't over yet. He grabbed me from behind whilst bound and penetrated me deeply. It hurt with all of the clamps in place and the sensitivity of the electrical current, but he didn't care. He kept fucking me. But I couldn't feel anything but pain. Next thing he removed me from the strappado and threw me on the table; removing the clamps and gag in one foul swoop, he grabbed the pin nearby and pierced it straight through my nipple. "You want to refrain from pleasure?" he yelled. "Then I'll give you pain." He tied me to the cornices and exposed my clitoris, painfully biting and sucking it until it was red with achiness. "Will you cum now?" He threatened. I nodded, petrified of what could come next. He continued until my clitoris was big and red and I was beginning to tremble then right before I came he forced himself inside of me, hard and fast and even though I had cum and it was painful, he kept going for what seemed like hours until he too came. It was almost like he was holding out on me, making it hard so that I could be in much more pain.

Obviously, I wasn't rough enough with Rose and I really need to work on faking it so that I would never have to go through that again. This time he left me there chained to the bed. I was abandoned unlike the usual case with Sabe coming in, and I felt completely exposed; besmirched.

It kept me thinking at least. Was it the fact that he hadn't been with me for over three days? The effects of the soon-to-be war? My performance? Or all three in existence? Who was to know, and he wasn't going to tell me. Soon, I began shivering and I could feel the blood sticking to my body. I was encompassed in pain, but I couldn't, for all of my senses, work out specifically where any of it was coming from. My vagina was throbbing, and my clitoris seized with agony, but they were the least of my troubles. The violent sex had further embedded the scarring from the whips on my back and soon enough, to my pleasure, I had passed out from the pain.

I must have been out to it for at least half the day because it was nightfall before Sabe came in – Ario at her side. They removed my chains and I let them puppet me around as for that moment my spirit and physical strength had completely left me. They put me into the bath of aloe and immediately, I sprung to life with the immense torment of it all. They had to scrub harder than usual because the blood had set into my wounds and this made me wince and shudder at the same time. Ario was not as soft as Sabe but I think that was the intention of it all.

Kemp left me lying in the cage for days, still confused by what had happened. At least Rose was nearby to keep me company. He must have at least liked it somewhat or else she would have become someone else's pet by now. She was put in a cage next to mine and the Razors at the door were multiplied. I'm guessing because Kemp had left to start the raids on any of the 'outlaw' Razor camps; with one intention, Intel and to kill them all.

Chapter 5

Spring was approaching so it was much easier to find ground cover and with the Intel from Rachel, Kemp knew exactly where Peter's site was. But if his scouts had returned then they would be on the move and this is where my brother's unit would come into it. They lived in the trees and were extremely efficient scouts – usually navigating by the stars – something that Chase had learnt as a child – and lay dead still during the days; ever watching for nearby camps. The reports that returned were of an ex-Razor camp found where Peter had been so this made the journey much harder. I just hoped that Chase would come back safely to me, unscathed and having completed his mission because Kemp hated failure and it would reflect not only on the community but on me as well.

Meanwhile Rose and I had begun to chat, lightly at first but then she began telling the stories of what the Razors had done to her community. She commenced by saying that she was out in the fields, which was lucky because she was on the east side and they approached from the west. She hid down amongst the wheat stalks and from there she could see the torment of her people. It was much the same story as mine, but she was not able to see her family at all. She had three sisters, along with her mum and dad. So, you only could imagine what they went through or where they ended up as all of the women would have been taken hostage. Her sisters were 16, 14 and 12, so the Razors would have taken advantage of every moment and by the looks of Rose, they would have all been taken into slavery as pets. As for her father, he would have become the main meal and her mother much like my own.

Rose explained it from the point of view of the screaming that she could hear; constant, differing pitches and shouting of commands from the Razor leaders. This infuriated me, and she could tell I was getting agitated. Gunshots sprung out (which was unusual for a Razor clan; Peter perhaps?) then it all went silent. Rose said this is when she made a break for it. She had heard of this place called Blood Stone which was a sacred site that no one went to but before she knew it a group of scouts had captured her bringing her straight to Kemp. Which in turn was lucky because her fate would have been sealed right there out in the woods if they hadn't made that choice. It would have been Chase's troops, I imagine.

She recalled how Kemp looked her up and down with envious eyes and commanded for her to be left alone and encamped in another cage in the tent next door to mine with militants guarding her. She was ordered not to be touched. She was there for days before we met, and Kemp would visit her watching her, intimidating her and then leave just as silently as he came. He was prepping her, but she didn't know it at the time.

Rose spoke to me about her husband for the first time on the third day. How they were so deeply in love and had only been married a few months before the Razors had invaded. Unfortunately, he was in camp at the time, so she was still unaware of what had happened to him. For all she knew he was dead, but I knew better – they had probably taken him through the intensive training, but I wasn't going to tell her that. It was still early days. Rose and I grew to love each other, as sisters and we would try and make light of any situation through making jokes, laughing and telling stories of the past, much to the dismay of the guards. I felt almost normal again, after being alone for such a long time.

It was less than a week when the camp moved into action; an obvious sign that the Razors had returned. My anxiety spiked because I knew Kemp was back and I didn't know what mood he was in. Plus, I was still recovering from our last encounter. It wasn't long before he entered our tent; moodily stared through me looking scarred and bloody but he then left almost as quickly as he came. That's when my conversations with Rose became more serious. I told her about what had happened last time and that if we were to be together again that I would need to do some things to her that are against my nature; she understood, but I carried this inner turmoil because we had become so close that I didn't want to hurt her. We talked about maybe being more passionate towards each other and having spent days together I kind of felt a kinship with her anyway. I wanted to protect her just as much as she wanted to be protected. And if that meant we needed to act in a certain way then that's just the way that it would have to be.

The raid must have been a success because the camp was back in full swing and there was talk of Peter being held hostage in a nearby cage; apparently not in the best condition. Also, Kemp had managed to murder every last one of Peter's camp which would send out a message not only to the other

Razors that were plotting against Kemp but to the Theodoris who were attempting to take over the camp.

Every now and then Rose and I could hear screams coming from Peter and it was obvious that they were working him over, torturing him and then allowing him time to recuperate before doing it all again. A method used more than once by this Razor colony. I couldn't see what was happening, but I'd seen it all before and if they hadn't used the truth serum on him yet, Kemp was definitely pissed.

It was another day before Kemp came in to see us. He eyed me maliciously. I was his prey. It seemed as though Rose would not be taking part in today's ritual. I could tell he was still angry from our last encounter and after the last massacre, he was looking for blood. I could almost taste it on his breath as he dragged me by my hair out of the cage. He didn't bother to prepare me this time but rather bent me over the table, lifted my dress, stroked himself until he was fully erect and fucked me until he had cum in violent force. He then threw me back in the cage, leaving without a word. By now I was used to this, but it still hurt deep inside and I sat quietly for the next few hours. I could tell Rose wanted to say something but being discerning of my mood she refrained and we both sat in silence. For the first time, I started to cry, hunched over in the corner of my cage. It was a wonder this had not happened sooner but now I could not stop it; my everything had been taken from me and I felt like the whore he had called me a few days ago.

This series of fucking for his self-gratification went on for about a week before he began to speak to me again. Rolling me onto my back he gnarled at me and said, "Are you ready?" Ready for what I was thinking but deep down I knew it was now my time to perform and there was no way I was messing it up this time.

Kemp called for four of his men to arm the tent as I said that I would need the freedom to do whatever I liked. "This is going to hurt," I whispered regretfully to Rose, and she managed a scared smile back at me.

"Whatever you need to do," she replied unknowingly; for she knew what would happen to me if I didn't perform to Kemp's – and the other onlookers' – standards.

They had laid out a variety of items besides the table, including restraints, knives, gags and the like. All I had to do was to choose wisely. I told her that we needed to be seductive – to look like we were in pain and enjoying it at the same time; just to get through the next few hours. This time, Kemp did not sit back but rather participated fully in this threesome. From the beginning, I was wild with intent – I grabbed Rose and kissed her profusely while pulling her in close to me. We made out while Kemp started biting and licking my neck and caressing my breasts. He would move between my breasts and Rose's until both of our bodies betrayed us; nipples standing on end taut and swollen. The men behind watched on as we, in one sense, began to seduce each other.

That was until, without noticing, Kemp grabbed the whip and belted me hard from behind. It startled me so much that I bit Rose on the lip, and she was bleeding profusely. Obviously, it was not yet rough enough for him. I laid Rose down while he continued to whip me and took the candlewax from the side table dripping the hot wax over her body. Kemp pushed my head into her vulva and coerced me to begin licking her wildly while he continued to whip my backside getting Ario to continue with the waxing. We performed well, groaning, moaning and whimpering at all the right times, or so we thought. My back and buttocks were now a mess of blood and Rose was covered in wax. Kemp laid me on my back and pulled down the cage of spikes on me and made me watch as he bent Rose over the side of the table and belted her hard with a cane. I cringed, and she screamed. Trying to move was in vain as the spikes only further ripped at my abdomen. He then commanded her to go down on me while he bit my nipples hard before clamping them with the steel pegs. Moving in behind Rose he started to bite her buttocks, bruises were already starting to form. Underneath her, he toyed with her turgid clitoris, but she kept moving too much so he chained her to the cornices by her ankles. He commanded Ario to place the chords from the battery on my nipples and at a low voltage, he set them off sending an electric current through my body and into Rose's. Both of us squealed and it was not in delight.

Pushing her head further into my vagina, he commanded Rose to lick me out and Ario again set off the electric pulse, making both of us scream as our bodies contorted. Kemp then brought out something I had never seen before. It vibrated in his hand and after spitting on it he inserted it into Rose. She squirmed with guilty pleasure and I could see her beginning to tremble. She was losing all sense of consciousness, but I was wet enough by then for Kemp to tie my wrists to the top two cornices and remove the cage. It was then that I noticed that this thing had two sides. He took Rose and forced her inside of me. The vibration caught me by surprise, and I had to stop myself from immediately cumming. Then Kemp hovered above me, he did not have to say the words. I knew what he wanted me to do, so I focused on that instead of the pleasure I was gaining from Rose fucking me from below. I knew that we all had to come together or else there would be hell to pay.

The problem was that Rose was coming quicker than Kemp and me. I eyed her off, but Kemp kept pushing her downwards, his arms solidly locking her shoulders in. "You better be quick," he warned and with that I sucked harder and harder, manoeuvring my tongue around his glands. He was solitarily full and beginning to moan and all I could think was, 'Thank fuck for that' because I didn't know how much longer I could have held off. The problem was that Rose couldn't, she started quivering violently and came well before Kemp and I. Angrily, Kemp threw her from the bed, painfully reefing the piece out of me he started vigorously fucking me, with the warning that I had better come at the same time as him. I held out and held out until finally his groaning got louder and louder and I released just as he came, but as he did, he pulled out ejaculating all over my abdomen and continuing to masturbate and to ejaculate more until he was completely spent. To my surprise, he lay there for a moment and Rose and I dared not move. I felt completely numb, torn apart.

After the few days without him around, I had come to realise that he was only to become more violent as his psychopathic traits were leading to not only make me completely submissive but to take the very essence of my soul from me. It must have been a tough raid and he was certainly pissed about Peter and his alliance with the Theodoris.

Moments later, Ario came in and cleaned both Rose and me up. This time I didn't feel like talking. I lay slumped in the corner hugging the bar on the cage. All efforts on Rose's behalf to console me had been to no effect as I was in no mood to converse. Ario watched on from the entrance of the tent and I could see the lust in his eyes. Rose was soon escorted from the room and I was once again alone. But I didn't mind. I wanted it to be this way. I didn't want to know about the world around me. I even blocked out the mocking and screaming, retreating to my own mind as confused as it was. For days I lay there, refusing to eat or drink. I even refused Kemp's gaze when he entered the tent. I was traumatized and there was no way back from it. The darkness had encroached upon me and settled within my heart. He had beaten me. I was no longer any part of the person I used to be, only a shadow of my former self. With every move he made I lay there and just let him control me; a puppet in his hands; a play toy, but for how long could I let this go on?

It wasn't until Peter finally broke on where the others were camped that I started to think that this was my chance to escape because if I didn't soon, the escape plan would be made for me. I was going to kill myself. But how was I to escape? If he was away and all of the warriors were gone then perhaps, I could fight off a few of the guards, also, I had chipped slowly away at the corner of my cage and the hinges that held it together at the back were slowly easing. I knew it wouldn't be long before I could push through them. But I knew I needed to do it before Kemp decided to move base because for certain his minions would find the scraping that I was doing. It was only a small piece of brass that I was using but it was enough to file away at the iron joints.

The camp jolted to life and Kemp was again ordering his men and women into battle. They were to take out three Theodoris platoons and with them the three joint Razor camps in the next few days, so I knew that my time was short. I had to act now. I more vigorously filed at the hinges and managed to break one free. The other was more stubborn, plus with the guards checking on me all the time I didn't have much freedom on my escape. Finally, the other clamp had freed, and I sprung to life. Waiting for the guards to check one more time I pulled at the back of the cage and slid out under the back of the tent. I made a sprint for it, feeling sorry for Rose but unable to help her at this point in time. All I knew was that I needed to run as fast as I could, which was no easy task after being cramped up in a cage for such a long time. By the time I was out of reach further into the forest, the shouting had become weak, but the gunshots were loud and clear. I'm guessing they were meant for the guards.

I knew that Kemp's trackers would find me in an instant, so I needed to find water in order for them to lose my trail. I had heard of a spring nearby, so I ventured into a valley running to the sound of trickling water, which luckily turned out to be a waterfall. The shouting was getting closer and I knew that at one stage in my life I could swim so all I needed to do was jump. It must have been a twenty-foot drop and my legs were trembling, but anything was better than going back to that camp, back to Kemp. I counted down from three and just as I jumped gunshots rang out behind me.

The freefall felt like it was going on forever and I couldn't help but scream as I hit the water hard. It was like landing on solid ground and I was immediately pushed under by the force of the falling water. Rock upon rock hit me, thrusting me from one side to another and in between I could only get gasps of air as I was pulled up by the rapids. The bullets were skimming past me and it wasn't long before the troops were climbing down rocks in hot pursuit with commands forcefully protruding from Kemp's mouth. They knew their fate if they didn't bring me back, seemingly dead or preferably alive. I continued to be washed downstream through white water until I finally came to the calm water. Ironic really, as I was far from being calm. I made tracks along the water's edge to hide my footprints; with my body aching all over I knew that I could not outrun them, so I took refuge in an abandoned log within the forest, making sure to cover my tracks.

Soon enough, Kemp, followed by the other Razors, ran past pursuing what now was a ghost. I dared not move let alone let out a single breath. But it wasn't long before the backtracking began. They had realised I had not gotten that far, and the trackers were closing in on me. I could see them from the crevices in the open log and finally one caught my eye. "She's here," he yelled. Startling me into a full-blown, panic attack and before I knew it everything had gone black.

The next thing I knew I was in Rose's cage in her arms in the tent next to mine. I could hear welding from my tent and assumed that Smith was making my cage more foolproof. Kemp had left with the other warriors and the camp was quiet, apart from the two new guards sitting in the cage in front of us. We were not to be trusted and I knew Kemp was not going to risk the chance of me escaping again. I had a chronic headache; I assume from the butt of the gun that I had received to the head and there was more scarring on my body and I couldn't for the life of me remember where it had come from.

Chapter 6

Days went by before the Razors returned and there were many more captives, I would imagine leaders that were strung up beside what was left of Peter in the middle of base camp. Through the hole in the tent, I could count at least ten but there were more than that beyond my sight. Some Razors, some Theodoris, so they must have come upon more camps than expected. Kemp seemed content but still ordered the others around and Benedict was already preparing truth serums for their next raids. Kemp was relentless in exterminating every last one of them.

On one of my morning toilet runs, apart from the men tied up in the trees, I noticed that the camp's size had increased as more Razors joined Kemp's settlement and there were plenty more play toys for the Razors to manipulate. Upon return, I snuggled closer into Rose as the bossing around ceased and Kemp stood, his shadow filling the entrance to the tent. He had an obsessive desiring look on his face, but I could tell that he had taken a lot of his angst out on the raided women because he didn't come straight to us, rather he stood there glaring with intimidation. I shuddered and drew closer to Rose and she embraced me tightly. He was biding his time. What worse could he do to me?

Later that day, he came in and sat down beside me. "Have you ever wondered why you are mine?"

I must admit the thought had passed my mind on a number of occasions, but I knew that asking would not help.

For the first time, he began to open up to me.

"Your father was a Razor."

"Bullshit," I yelled confronting him.

He began to tell me the story of how my father, Jack, had taken him as a teenager and raised him to become a Razor much like himself. In the initial stages, Razors were there as an uprising to kill off the Theodoris camps and that was the main purpose of them. When Kemp was 15, Jack left the camp as the Razor's code had changed and he no longer wanted to be a part of it. It wasn't until years later Kemp had heard of Jack's settlement and of his family and that was the only reason why Chase and I were still alive until this day. Jack had to pay for what he had done in leaving the Razors, and his family – us – were just collateral in all of this.

I couldn't believe it and wouldn't believe it, Kemp was lying to me, playing games; it couldn't be true.

"Why do you think your father was such a good sharpshooter? But a pacifist? C'mon, that is the biggest contradiction I have ever heard of."

"It was his upbringing," I forced.

"Yeah, as a Razor," Kemp forced back. "This makes you Razor born."

I stopped, perplexed, there was no way this could be possible, he was playing with my mind and I had no explanation to prove otherwise. It was his word against my upbringing. Dad was good with a gun, but he used it to hunt rabbits and food for our colony, not people.

"Is this why Chase has been trained for you to be a sharpshooter?"

Kemp nodded.

"So why keep me here?"

"You are a solid reminder of the betrayal of your father. This is your destiny. And mine. We were always meant to be married, it was a promise of the elders at the time, but your father refused and snuck away with you all before it could be unified. Why do you think I waited so long to be with you? Why do you think that I try to get you to 'free yourself' so that we can finally make love?"

I protested, "You are incapable of making love, you are a psychopath."

I sensed a glint in his eyes, but also a signal of truth. He wasn't lying and if this was the truth then what did that mean for me? For him? For Chase? My mother?

"The training is part and parcel of being a Razor," he explained. "True submission."

I was banging on the bars now, crying, "What makes you think that I can trust you?"

That's when he brought in Ben. I vaguely remembered him from my childhood (conflicting me) until it all came flashing back to me; the camps the movements, my father yelling orders. But no, it was my mind deceiving me. I must have wiped it from my memory. Soon the apothecary came in and gave both Ben and me the truth serum. Ben reflected on the early days when we were really young. I would have been about six and he led with how my father had taken his group of 'Settlers' captive before training him to become a Razor. Kemp was also one of these boys who watched on as his family was tortured and strung to bleed out above him.

"It was your father that made me who I am today. He taught me everything I know."

It was all coming back to me. I remembered Kemp as a scared boy and even though I was hidden from the violence, through the gaps in the tent my brother and I could still see what was happening to their families.

"Does Chase know?"

"Yes."

Scepticism played on my mind but I knew that under the truth serum, my memories were true so how could I fight them?

This would explain Kemp's obsession but not his behaviour.

"It is just a pity that I am desensitised to falling completely in love now. It has been beaten out of me, but I can't let go of you. Your pain is my pleasure and your pleasure, my pain. We have always been destined to be together."

My head was spinning, and I was trying to fight the serum. I didn't know what to make of this. Of Ben. Of Kemp. My life had been tipped upside down and now my thoughts began racing. I am a Razor and a Settler? Or am I even defined by either of these? It explains his obsession and why I am 'his'. We were consummated the first time we slept together. The only thing is that he sees me as his possession, something to be owned, rather than unified. But is that his fault, or the training, the act of trying to survive in this world of chaos? Obviously, if my father trained him, he taught him well. But how could I be in love with a psychopath? Someone who wants to love me and hurt me all at the same time? And where does Rose fit into all of this?

"What about Rose?" I blurted out.

"She is what is needed to tame you; to keep you in my control. Don't you get it? Without her and your love for her, I could lose you forever. I can't help what I have become but at least together you can help me to understand love more."

What the fuck was he talking about? I wasn't in love with Rose and Rose wasn't in love with me… or were we? We had become more intimate over the last few weeks and through our own explorations Kemp had become more jealous, and of course, there was this never-ending need to protect her, to my demise. Fuck!

Benedict soon came in with this drug that I had never seen before and Kemp made both Rose and I drink it. The potion created euphoria in me, and I could see that Rose was tightening around me. Before long, we were making full-scale passionate love. Was this Kemp's proof to me? Or was he coercing me into believing his lies? I could never tell but my want for Rose and Kemp became insatiable.

We wrestled on the table taking turns in erotically kissing, licking and touching each other. There was no zone untouched and I could tell that all three of us were enjoying this. I was not scared but rather wanted more. The morning had soon gone, and we had the ability to have multiple orgasms throughout the day. I was in my element. I spent most of my time with Rose licking her pussy and caressing her breasts in acts of love. Kemp added to the threesome playing with me, seducing my inflamed anus and slipping in and out of my suddenly eager vagina, creating electrifying pulses of energy. We were one. Every anxiety had left me, and we threw each other madly from one position to the next engaging in full-scale pleasure. It was the most intense experience of my life and I did not want it to stop, ever.

Kissing passionately, we moved from neck to hips, to lips, spiritedly guiding each other through every moment. Kemp threw me on the table and directed Rose to passionately kiss his neck and back while he deliberately played with my vulva, lifting the hood to my bulging clitoris and allowing me to reach the point of coming then drawing back to do the same with Rose. I was then under the instruction to suck his crazed and vivacious cock and again he pulled away before the vibrations made him come. We were in a state of bliss.

When the afternoon sun was setting, Kemp swung into action holding my arms above my head, directing Rose to kiss me passionately while he bit my neck and slowly, he penetrated me, teasing me for what seemed like hours before bringing me to the ultimate orgasm. But he did not stop there – he was intent on making me cum over and over again, so he moved me to my side and whilst Rose was licking my vulva, Kemp was taking me from behind. I came again. Passionately kissing Rose, he moved to fuck her too and soon she came under the throbbing weight of his penis. But he was not yet finished. Rose was instructed to lay on the bed while he inserted the vibrating stick into her and from above, I passionately kissed her and embraced her breasts while Kemp tilted my head back and fucked me from behind. Pulsing from the inside I tried to prevent myself from coming but seeing Rose lose control made me lose focus and we all came in one grand gesture.

Slumped over one another, I immediately fell asleep, embraced by Rose and Kemp, watched by Ario and before I knew it, morning had come, Kemp was gone, and both Rose and I were again chained by our ankles to the cornices of the bed. We lay holding each other, relishing the fact that we could finally rest, still feeling euphoric from the drug gone yesterday. I gazed into Rose's eyes and at that moment I realised that Kemp was right. I was in love with her. And at that moment I knew that nothing else mattered.

It had taken one day for us to realise the fullness of what was happening between us. I couldn't leave her again. We were bonded and there was nothing that could release me from the fullness of this love. Kemp's plan had worked. He had emotionally coerced me into a love so deep that I knew that I could never leave without her and of course, he had another crutch for me to do whatever he wanted.

Lying on that table Rose and I made love multiple times, softly and sweetly, with Ario's eyes ever watching us. But I did not care; we were devoted in spirit, soul and body. Kemp strategically left us for a few days before entering the tent again. At this point, it was dark and we were deeply asleep in each other's arms. I sensed him move towards us and with his light touch upon me, I jumped, waking Rose from her sleep. He took Rose and locked her in the cage. He was horny, I was confused but I could feel the stiffness of his penis under his linen pants. At this point, I didn't want him; I wanted Rose and protested as he lubricated me from below. It was hard and fast and then he left just as quickly as he had come; confusing me even more. Ario was ordered to leave me there and over the next few days, Rose was made to look on as he continued to fuck me, and then leave; some days on several occasions in between his political endeavours. What pained me more was that I couldn't touch Rose. And his pervasive nature had become clear. I was his. Rose was only secondary to his explorations and now I was emotionally attached he knew that I would do anything for her, including not escaping without her.

Both Rose and I were taken outside the next day and as the sun glistened off the dew-covered nearby leaves; I couldn't help but squint at the sun's morning brightness. I was still stiff from being locked in the cage but at least Rose and I had kept our exercising a high priority, so I wasn't too uneasy on my feet. It looked like we were on the move again and this time Kemp was not letting either of us out of his sight, but I didn't care, I was taking in all that 'outside' life had to offer. The brilliant hues and smells of the flowers; at first it was overwhelming, and I wanted to be put back in my cage, safe and sound, but before long I had become one with my environment and began to appreciate the business of the camp.

The camp was a bustle of noise and movement, with orders coming from all around. The acclimatisation of movement was second nature to the Razors in Kemp's ground now and each knew their place extremely well, but with so many new Razors there was a lot of 'following' going on as the newbies copied eagerly what the elders were doing. We had a new Smith in our midst, called Shade and a new apothecary called, Aaby; she was the first female (apart from Sabe who needed no formal training) that I had heard of. Amongst the rest, there were training warriors, snipers, archers, craftspeople and many more. This mini-society was functioning at optimum and it was moving quickly.

We headed west along the waterfall's edge and within half a day the scouts had found a new destination for us. It was a lot smaller than usual but these days we were the target, so we needed more coverage and security than ever. Setting up base Rose and I were taken to have our first bath in a nearby stream. Weirdly the cool running water tingled my skin and the rocks and sand below acted as exfoliation. It was a playful endeavour for us both as we bathed each other; with only the small amounts of light glistening from above. It was then that I noticed a plane in the sky; small but recognisable. Kemp and Ario pulled us in under the cover and these were the first signs that the Theodoris were wasting the well-coveted aviation fuel that there was left to find us. Luckily, we were well hidden. It just meant no campfires for at least a couple more nights and more scout patrols in order to keep our borders secure. Training was in full swing and whoever didn't meet the cut was sentenced to kitchen duties or the like. It was only the best that Kemp was interested in and if this meant combining with more Razor warriors then this was what was going to be. Men and women flocked from nearby sites and the training was upped. Even Rose and I were beginning to participate in the training, in case of a nearby raid. Kemp couldn't be too careful.

He kept me away from Chase even though being a sniper was the most complimentary to my method of thinking, so we were placed under Transit for close combat training and started our physical conditioning to mimic his styles of battle. At first, it was intense physical training, rebuilding the muscle tone that we had lost over the many months of isolation. It took weeks of this intense physical activity to get us into a pace that was even remotely close to Transit. A lot of the training also involved camouflage and resistance training (although we had endured enough of that already). We were given truth serum and made to withstand the vicious attacks and mental torments of the Razor militia. By nightfall, we were happy to be back in our cages, but what I still could not understand was that Rose and I were such a flight risk so why spend so much time investing in getting us ready for warfare?

We must have made the cut though because the next morning we were back into it in full swing. It seems we were both naturals, of course, I knew why I was, but Rose? Today we started weapons training – we weren't allowed real knives of course but we were asked to engage in close combat and taught the art of the melee. A quiet and really effective takedown, one I would never forget. We also learnt how to choke someone out and continued with the fundamental Razor fighting techniques. We were not allowed to know much in the form of Intel but every now and then we would be close enough to hear of another Razor attack or at the least the formation of more alliances. There must have been over 20 leaders present at one stage which was valuable because it kept Kemp extremely busy and allowed for Rose and me to spend more time together, which bizarrely enough I needed. It wasn't long before our training had taken us to new heights, and we were using rubber bullets and wooden arrows to take down targets. Kemp had an obvious purpose for us, but I still couldn't gage whether it was strategic or psychological; whatever the case we were outside of the cage and learning the valuable skills that all should know in order to keep from being taken captive by the other anti-Kemp Razor clans, or their Theodoris allies.

Rose and I were becoming quite crafty in the skills of warfare and I was remembering back to my days when my father had taught me a thing or two about defending, attacking and escaping – the bare necessities – which I was to take full advantage of in Kemp's next raid.

Chapter 7

Kemp had left with many of the troops leaving Ario in charge of us. I had noticed a certain rising lust in Ario's eyes so when the next raid came, I called him close to the cage Rose and I were entrapped in. Exposing myself to him I swore I would never tell if he wanted us to be with him. Ario flinched but as Rose followed my lead it proved too much for him and soon enough, he had the cage opened and pulled me close to him. I moved into a quick passionate kiss and gestured with my hand for Rose to grab the key. With his attention solely on me, it was a piece of cake and within seconds I had turned him to kiss the back of his neck and choked him out with the now unfixed chain from our ankles.

We slipped under the back of the tent and made a quick run for it. With our newly found stamina and camouflage skills we were well away from camp before morning. We scarred ourselves through thistles four feet in size and managed to find the perfect hiding spot for the day. We knew that Ario would have risen only moments later but without Kemp there I knew we were only safe to move around of a night.

We could hear search parties throughout the day, but no one was going to venture into the thistles. We remained silent for what seemed like an eternity. The only problem was where to next? I had heard of nearby settlements but that would be the first place that they would look. For now, we were on our own, but at least we had each other.

Two days had passed, and we had moved a fair way on foot, which was enough to put Kemp's camp behind us, but his scouts were highly skilled so wherever we could we would use the rivers and dense forest as our guide. It wasn't long before I read a tattered sign; this place was called Lensil back in the day and all I knew was that according to the stars we were continuing to head east. Luck had found us here as there was plenty of water, animals and fish to catch. We found a forgotten waterfall with just a big enough gap behind it to hide the two of us and began feasting on the abundance of berries, fish and wallabies. After three days of wandering, we finally found a place of refuge where we knew that we would be safe enough to rest.

I must have slept for hours as I awoke to Rose gone and immediately flew into a panic. Had she been found? I dared not move for it was the middle of the afternoon and there was no way I was going back to the wrath of Kemp and his men for I was sure that this time I would not survive it. I decided to wait until nightfall, but Rose returned shortly before then.

"Jesus, girl, where have you been?"

"Scouting," was her response.

Scouting, in daylight?

"What if you had been taken?"

"I heard some children nearby playing in the pool of the lower waterfall and I freaked out. I thought that they were Razor kids, but it turns out that there is a settlement nearby. So, I sought them out. They are well armed and have set up in this place; almost like a fortress. I watched from the heights of a nearby tree. They are a settlement of course and a well-set up one."

I knew it wouldn't be long before Kemp got the scent of our trail and sent one of his groups of scouts our way; so, I had this sudden sense of urgency to warn these people of their impending doom; because according to Rose, although well-armed – they were no match for the 20 odd Razor groups on a rampage of nearby 'Settlers', 'Razors' or 'Theodoristes'. We waited until sundown and moved towards the settlement. They were in full swing and Rose was right – this was more like an army base camp than a settlement. I knew that we needed to approach with caution, but how do we gain their trust? It is unlikely that they would let us step foot inside of the fortress let alone seek solitude. But what other choice did we have?

We moved to the main gate and immediately all eyes, guns and arrows were upon us.

A loud shout came from the gateway, "Stop right there."

"Please hear me out," I called back.

He continued, "If you take one step further, I will shoot you right where you stand."

I needed to up the ante. I could have been killed for this, but I pulled down my shirt to reveal the gold ring around my neck and yelled, "We have been slaves of Kemp for many years, we only seek solitude; a word with your leader."

I could hear muffled sounds and arguing followed by an anxious voice saying, "What if they have led them here?"

Finally, a thin tall man came to the gate and beckoned us closer. "How far away are they?" he questioned.

"I'm not sure, but we have been running and hiding for days and have not seen any of his scouts for at least two days."

The man thought intently and examined the gold around my neck. I knew what he was thinking. If Kemp was close then at least we could be used for leverage, but I didn't care, anything was safer than being alone.

Much to the guard's astonishment, and my own, he let us in but much like Kemp's camp we were chained up but not before being checked for monitors. This was no average settlement. I could tell, they were much more organised than the others that I had seen and were definitely not pacifists. They were willing to fight for their freedom. Which suited both Rose and me well. Even though chained up I was still happy to be free from the demon and his psychopathic men and for the one-minute moment, I'd even had the thought that they may have given up the search. It would be half a day when gunshots rang out and a group of Razors had stumbled upon the settlement. They didn't last long though between the sharpshooters, the archers and the camouflaged men who seemed to come out of nowhere, and soon enough each was buried in a mass grave well beyond the fortress.

It was lucky that Jevers, the leader of this settlement, knew this group of Razors was not that of Kemp's, as they had attempted to dethrone them on numerous occasions only to fail and try again; after regrouping what was left of them. Jevers sent out his own platoon of scouts to make sure that their Razor camp was completely annihilated, and they didn't have to deal with the annoyance of their return.

Soon he was on Rose and me, scowling; I knew what he was thinking, and I was thinking how stupid I had been to take us there. He eyeballed me and we were interlocked in a challenge of wits until Jevers was called away by his offsiders. I was wrong, this was no point of solitude just another place that we needed to escape and the worst of it was that we had put all of these people at risk.

Jevers upped the ante and the camp had swung into full combat mode. From what I could see through the gates just shy into the forest unearthed, there was an entrance to an underground burrow, somewhere it linked to inside the fort and I'm sure according to these Settlers there were more. Within an hour the children were relocated, and everyone was on watch. I had not seen anything like it. These people have obviously been through a lot and their leaders; very smart.

Jevers was watching me closely and had soon realised that I was casing the place and Rose and I were promptly moved to a tent. From there we could only hear voices of the outside world and every now and again a few bowls of food would come through a gap in the tent.

It would be another ten days before the first gunshot would go off.

Within those ten days, Rose and I had the freedom to love freely and safely. We were left alone. It was maybe the third night when we began to become physically close again. We were talking about some of our childhood memories when I found myself being seduced by her beautiful pools of blue eyes. I came in slowly kissing her gently on the lips almost mid-conversation. I didn't want to talk. I wanted more than ever to be with her. Caressing her long brown hair and kissing her gently I couldn't help but pull her closer to me. I could feel her pulsing heart against my chest and she began to kiss me harder, pulling me towards her breasts. I pulled her shirt over her head and wrapped around each other we began to make love. Sweet, soft, delicate love. I had fallen for her and her, for me. Stroking her breasts lightly they came to life and in response, my body was covered with goosebumps. Moving gently down her neck and collarbone, I encouraged her nipples further with my lips. In response, she groaned and all I wanted at that moment was to show how much I really cared for her. There was not one part of her that was untouched. My favourite part of her, the place inside of her hip bone I spent moments teasing her, using my fingertips to lightly feel her, to really connect. It wasn't long before she was begging for me to touch her below.

I kissed her gently on the lips and without taking my eyes off of hers I moved directly to her clitoris swirling my tongue around the outsides and under her delicate hood; building her up until she was beautifully red and huge with desire. She clenched her hands beside me pulling at the hay and arching her back; all the while moaning with quiet pleasure. I could feel the heat rise inside of her and for the first time in a long time, I genuinely smiled. I quickened the pace making slow upward movements from her vagina, flicking my tongue over her pulsing clitoris, Rose was beginning to tighten and just as she was about to come I took my fingers and pushed hard into her G spot, and before I knew it through breathless and intense motion she came; her body trembling over and over again. It wasn't until then I slowly withdrew and kissed her gently all the way to her lips where we lay beside each other, speechless, looking into each other's eyes. There were no words needed and for seven more days, it was nothing but bliss for us. It was like nothing in the world even mattered, just our moments together, however brief they were to be.

At sundown was when the assault began. I knew deep inside this was no ordinary attack. I could feel the fear rise within. Kemp was out there somewhere. And if Kemp was there it meant that even with the fortress and the fully trained army within, they were no match for the alliance that was inbound. My only solace was knowing that they had removed the children. The shouting continued after the gunshots and both sides were in full-scale combat. I tried to close my ears to the death that was happening all around us, within minutes they had penetrated the gates and the battle was continuing inside the fortress. The Settlers were losing.

"Where is she?" I heard his booming voice ring out over the others. "I know she's here. We tracked her here. Where is she?"

Soon after the fire began and all around, the tents were alight with the blaze. It was gaining on us and we were bound, but at least we had each other. I covered Rose's ears and we closened. It wasn't long before a shadow burst through the entrance of the tent. Wielding a knife, she came closer. "You brought this upon us."

I retaliated, "And you think that you would have been safe forever? Here in this fortress, now tomb?"

I had offended her and though angry, the tent had started burning around us and she undid our chains, "Run."

We didn't need a moment, the surprise leapt us to life and within steps we were out of the fortress and running into the bush but not before Transit spotted us. "Over there. The rabbits."

I could hear Kemp's orders; he sent a band of his crew out to follow us. We tailed it but after being couped up for so long I found it hard to stay on my feet and with the forest proving difficult to navigate, I found myself tripping, Rose and I trying to keep each other going; to stay in front of the Razors. Before long they were on either side, ready to flank us. Arrows whizzed past my head, but I knew Kemp would not want us dead. Where would the pleasure be in that?

I ducked and weaved, and the night nature somewhat sprung to life. I was startled by an owl unusually lifting from the ground not perched in a tree. It frightened me into action, and everything began to slow down. It was as if my senses were sharpened and I could see every route clearly. I led Rose deeper into the unknown and even though the foot soldiers were hot on our trail I felt as though there was no one else there but Rose and me. The adrenaline had kicked in and there was no way of stopping us, or so I thought.

It wasn't until I felt the thick blood seep down my leg that I realised that an arrow had gone straight into my calf, wedged in deep and as soon as I noticed, the pain seared my brain and in a battle of mind versus body I pushed on. On my right flank, I noticed Transit gaining ground, he was a skilled huntsman so at this moment I knew that my hope needed to be stronger than my logic. But it was to no avail as an arrow pierced Rose and she dropped to the ground behind me. I tried to pull her up, but she had an arrow wedged in her upper thigh. Embedded deep. They were on us in seconds. All I could do was cover Rose as the assault began. First came a right hook, my head betrayed me and to no avail, I tried to shake the concussion. A kick to the side, and then four or more of them were on top of us. We were literally beaten into submission. Before I knew it, they were dragging us back to the fortress. Under the messiness of my mind fighting to stay alert, I could hear the war cry of Kemp's team and I knew that it was over.

Transit cried back and I could already feel the contempt in Kemp's psyche. I started to shake all over, and my legs gave way below me. The sound of his voice is all it needed to entrap me. It wasn't until they chained me up that I realised that Rose was gone. I began to panic. What were they doing to her? Was she still alive? It was then that I heard the sound of a piercing scream come from beyond me. I knew immediately it was her and it had at least answered one of my questions – for now. An opaque bag was placed over my head and before I knew it, I was kneeling but not for long as my senses gave way and I lay in the dirt with the memory of Rose's screams ringing through my ears.

It would be hours before I would be forced awake – ice cold water thrown over me startled me and I began to wriggle but in failure, without my hands, eyesight and the still all-consuming fuzziness I struggled to get to my knees. But that wasn't the purpose anyway. Two sets of arms wrapped around me and I was pulled upwards aggressively and the bag was pulled from my face. The screams were just a distant memory now and as I slowly looked up there was Kemp.

His eyes were burning with anger, he slapped me hard against my cheek and again I fell to the dust. I did not want to move from this place but again I was forced to my knees.

"Took you long enough." The words had escaped without thought and this time his foot connected with my stomach. Doubled over, I reckoned with myself to try and not provoke him. Not at this time anyway for he was in far from a playful mood. And I really should have known better, but my judgement was clouded by the pounding and aching I was now starting to feel as if my adrenals had failed me, and my nervous system was in full swing. I never learn. "Where's Rose?" I demanded, slurring my words as they came out.

He snarled at me and was quick to reply, "Far from you." Then he nodded to the men to chain me to the nearest post. Immediately I was forced back to the moments I first met Kemp, the day he ordered the slaughtering of my dad, turning my brother into a Razor and taking my mother as a play toy. I shook my head, physically trying to remove the memories from my consciousness, but it was no good, they kept at me and I felt myself starting to panic, my breath quickening and fear filling me almost to paralysis. I watched on as the Razors continued to set up camp and appropriated the remaining survivors through their normal rituals. I could feel it rise faster than I could compute and before I knew the substance came from my stomach and continued to pulsate through as vomit protruded from my mouth. It was too much to handle and my physical self-had taken over. I had passed out.

Chapter 8

Soon enough I awoke, more screams rained from behind me. I couldn't see Kemp and that was worse than knowing where he was. Again, I knew that voice. A pole was suspended just metres from me and she, Rose was chained to it naked, bruised and scared. I struggled against my chains and continued until my wrists were bleeding trying to get to her. Two men held me back. Frustrated, Kemp watched on as we looked into each other's eyes. I mouthed, I love you and she mouthed it back and that is when Kemp sprang into action. He sent four men to her and using a nearby fire and a branding stick they began to torture her, burning her body and making her do unsightly things. All I could do was watch on as they brutally began raping her, one after the other, sometimes more than one and it was at that moment that I began to weep, I called for her, I begged Kemp.

"Please stop, please. I will do anything! Kemp!"

His eyes stayed fixed on Rose and with a writhed smile he took pleasure in what was unfolding before me. Two more men came in and started beating her in between the fucking and the branding for what seemed like hours. Rose had become weak and limp. Finally, Kemp ordered her to be suspended by her arms from the pole and they began to build a wood stack below her.

My eyesight was starting to blur as my right eye started to bulge through the beating it had received earlier but I still would not take my eyes off of her. By now she was looking back at me, but I could tell her soul had almost drained from her. My mind flooded with thoughts from the past. Rose and I had become so close; every kiss, every touch, her blue eyes looking into mine; into each other's soul. I had fallen for her and now she was falling because of me. I remembered the conversation that we'd had. Because of what had happened to her family she wanted a proper burial; to be fully formed just like when she had begun as a fully formed human being. Were they going to take this from her too?

I watched as the Razors started to set up camp and scout groups were sent out to man the trees and find resources for the camp. They had enough hostages if it were to come to that, but Kemp was more interested in a different sort of live game. The first scouts came back in the first couple of hours with the first feast, while Rose was still hanging there. I was starting to get confused. Was this just another one of Kemp's tactics? It would be another couple of hours before another group returned with Chase in the lead. From what I could see his disposition was calm which meant that there wasn't a threat nearby but after a short meal his team was sent back out into the forest. The camp was sparse which meant that we were not going to be here for long, but time was of the essence, for Rose anyway. I was in luck; I found a piece of thin metal on the ground and was slowly trying to pick the lock. Without drawing too much attention to myself, I tried to writhe the lock-free, but it was to no avail as time was not on my side.

The sun was beginning to set, and the two men returned with three more men grabbing Rose from her post and dragging her to a nearby tent. It wasn't long before I heard the screams return again and I felt the anger rise from within. What was Kemp playing at? With his stupid games! I tried to cover my ears, but the chains were too tight. I could no longer bear the thought of what was happening to her or what was to come.

The men unchained me from the tree and moved me to a nearby tent and all I could do was lay there – exhausted from the day, I was defeated and before I knew it the sun pierced through the tent opening waking me to a new dawn. Most of the camp was in action and starting to pack for the next move. Chase was still nowhere to be seen but the other two scout groups were perched on the fortress walls with the others. What was weird was that a small group of Razors began to congregate in the square and more joined as the camp was locked and loaded for travel. Ario and another man came and dragged me back out to the tree. This time they held the chains and forcefully pushed me to my knees.

I could barely recognise her when they brought her out. The anger boiled inside me and I cursed Ario, trying to shake myself free, but they proved too strong for me. Rose was bloody and bruised all over. There was not a single part of her body left free from their assaults. Kemp nodded to the men and obediently they once again strung her from the pole but this time I recognised that they had added hay to the stack and my eyes widened in fear, my body tried with every ounce to get to her. "Rose!" I yelled. "Rose, keep your eyes on me." She was shaking all over too terrified to speak. A bag was placed over my head and the last thing I remember amongst the screams and the fire was that I could see her soul. I remembered her love and then I just broke down crying. I found myself in the dirt trying to make a sound but only managing to mouth the words, "No, no, I'm so sorry. I love you." And then she was gone. All went silent. I could feel my heart beating through my chest and they left me there to wait for the flames to die. My heart was as black as the ash that lay before me and my love was gone.

Once again, the numbness set in and it wasn't long before the Razor chanting began, and the taunting laughter rained throughout the campsite. Rose had but one wish; to be buried. The honour was not granted; she was burnt, and her ashes were scattered deep in the woods where I would never find her. I wish that Kemp had never found out. How could we allow ourselves to become so transparent? I felt the loneliness more than anything now. The days moulded, one into the other, my emotions; all but numb. I feel nothing. I act every day. I submit to everything. The fight is gone from me; even my brother seems like a complete stranger to me and what's even more alien is the desire in me to achieve nothingness.

Life is a challenge. I continue to try to believe in myself – to love myself but it is so hard to even connect within. I feel detached from the world around me, from life itself. I am the walking dead. People come and go – I engage but there is this acute sense of nothing being real; like it's all a dream and the worst part is that I feel like I won't ever wake up from this dream. I'm waiting for Abbot. Waiting to be found, when really, I need to find myself; I am all that is left. My brother has even abandoned me.

It is this truth deep within that I battle with on a regular basis – purpose – understanding – anything to resolve the pain and confusion that is ever so apparent in my life. It rises and

I fall, like the ebb and flow of the tide but like this, there are variables at play which are inconsistent all of the time. I never know what the waves will be like. It leaves me in a seasick state of mind and when I think I'm getting close to what I think is mastering one wave the water changes and with it the waves within the tides of time. Moment by moment, let alone day by day. It is a culmination of these ever-changing experiences which inhibit me from being able to maintain consistency and understanding in my life. With Rose gone, I feel like Alice down the rabbit hole, but with a much more painful outcome.

Kemp would come and visit me some nights, but he was cold, and his piercing eyes screamed at me at every moment. And every morning I would feel empty and ashamed. The physical wounds would heal but the psychological ones? I wasn't so sure anymore. He will never forgive me, and I just wanted to be left alone. The darkness sunk in as I realised that I am all alone with just my thoughts racing to keep me surviving. The trauma overwhelmed me and I became paralysed by the thoughts of years gone past. My youth was taken from me and this world is changing so drastically that fear is taking over every aspect of it.

We moved again, this time to a more deserted, rocky place. The area was sparse but beyond the rocks we were hidden within, you could see for miles. People from other camps would come and go but I had not the energy nor the concern to care about their presence. Kemp had more than this camp in this area. There were at least five other Razor camps along the outskirts acting as scouts which meant that even more were in the field. It was frightening to see how big they had become and even more frightening that I could see my brother changing each and every single day. He was one of them now. In fact, he wasn't just one of them but one of the best of them now. The enemy.

I could never imagine Chase being a leading scout in a Razor clan, but he had been completely indoctrinated. Sucked in by the acceptance he receives from this community turning a blind eye to all of the torture. He doesn't even communicate with me anymore, no eye contact, not even a smile; completely disassociating from me and by the look in his eye, life itself. I guess that's the way that he has learnt to survive; to justify his existence, his life. His main role is to scout, search and return with Intel or persons of interest. A lucky job really because he can somewhat block out what happens after she passes the buck.

There is this slight sense of guilt that I feel though, like a family guilt which arises because of a self-protective quality over the family name. Almost as if I am trying to protect what little is left of it, but I guess everyone knows who my dad was and that in itself has tainted the lives that we live today – even though he was trying so hard to move away from that existence. I was now not a Settler – nor would I ever succumb to being, a Razor, so what was I? At this point, it is way too much to think about and it is getting dark, so I try and fall asleep before Kemp arrives back at camp from his day scouting with the men and hope for the best.

I had the most vivid dreams last night. The first I was surrounded by a band of people who were all mentoring other people. They were working individually with them in each of their field areas and I was helping them, leading them. I knew exactly what to say and when and where each of them was in their processes. I felt liberated of sorts. Like I had found my calling and I wanted to stay in that dream forever. Rose was there and we were living a life of romance and that's when I called bullshit realising that it was just a dream.

85

Chapter 9

The next day news had come of my mother. It was not the kind of news any child would like to hear, and as I was taken to her memories of my childhood, flooded in her beautiful voice singing to me as a child, "Lavender blue dilly dilly, lavender green." Her smile as she would embrace me of a night and the warmth of her chest when I laid my head against her. The light shone in her eyes as she swished her hair from her face in the fields. She was even then more beautiful than anyone I'd ever seen. She would look at me and we would giggle about the silliest of things. She would tell me what stories she could remember of the old times. Tales of princesses and frogs that danced on lily pads. Nonsensical but nonetheless fun. I loved my mother and I hated them for taking those moments from me. They led me out to her, and she was laying there, skin and bones, but breathing ever so softly. She had aged beyond measure, but she had never lost her beauty. I asked for water and was allowed this one kind gesture and I nursed her head beckoning her to drink. She was frail but took small sips from my hands to her lips. Chase was soon there but distanced himself. He could not turn a blind eye now as it was staring him right in the face. Death.

Shallow breaths moved ever so slowly from her and I wanted nothing more than for her to live, but through all of the pain and hardship that she had been through I knew it would not be long before she would stop being the courageous woman that I had known and give in to the dust that surrounded her. I leaned in closer to feel the rise and fall of her chest like the old days and to feel the warmth of her breath on my head. She started to cough, and it was evident then through the blood that was coexisting with the oxygen from her lungs that there was no way back.

It would be hours before she passed, and I could not leave her side. It was almost as if, if I stayed, she could stay too, just that little longer. I whispered more than once, "I'm sorry, I love you, Mum, I love you." But even then, I knew it wasn't me that I was apologising for, but the extreme abuse that she had been under warranted it, at that moment. And then she was gone. Taken into the forest to her final resting place. Slipping from my mouth through sobs came, "No, no, Mum, no." But in my heart, I now knew that she was at peace.

There is a certain kind of jealousy that comes with death. It is so unknown and so peculiar that this parallel exists in our world. We yearn for it to end the pain but because of the reason for life, we hold on. We had lost track of age so many years before and all I knew was that she was young, too young for this to happen to her and even younger for her to have to endure so much pain and heartache. It was then that I finally reflected on how hard it must have been for her all of these years. How traumatic it all must have been, even with the death of Dad.

I could detach from these feelings but losing a partner and watching your family get destroyed was different. It made me think of Rose and the never-ending pain that enveloped my body, soul and spirit for so long and finally, I cried. An all-encompassing wailing came from within and the years of oppressed feelings finally were released. I was angry and warned through my eyes and body for no one to come near me. I pushed Chase away when he tried to console me and right to the core, I called him a 'traitor'. I must have yelled at him with every harsh cruel word I could think of. I hated him for what he had become, and he was here. What was he thinking? Cruelly I was pulled from my mother and made to watch as they took away her beautiful body. Through the anger, I held a proper memorial in my head and fantasised my way through it all. I would not let them beat me, not this time. She deserved better and even if it was all in my head, she would get it.

It was at this moment I had learnt to feel again. It was the death of Rose that made me numb, but now the death of my mother had unleashed in me an emotional whirlwind. I couldn't help but double up when the feelings would take over. I tried my best to distract, to push them away but they were uncontrollable. Unstoppable. They would take over everything in my inmost being until my heart would give in and the ache would sear through my body along with the tears that would flow from my eyes. The world would slow, and shadows would fill my mind; past, present or future, I didn't know. My mind had been filled with confusion and any sign of violence or death would throw me back into the chaos of my emotional pain. I had withdrawn from Chase and even though he would come to see me I would draw a blank and I still could not bring myself to look him in the eye let alone talk to him, even though I knew that none of this was his fault, that the position that he had been put in was also his method of survival. But my stubbornness could not allow me to feel that way. I just hoped that somewhere deep inside of him there was still the boy I knew from childhood, that it had not been completely taken from him.

That inevitable feeling that you need to be somewhere, but time is so elusive that you are caught up in the dream which exists in the now. That's what grief is like. Physiologically nothing can compare to the wretchedness of it all. How do you surpass the regret? The guilt? The pain? Stay longer with the good times, laughing and allowing myself to become engrossed in the brightness, sharing in the life that is now. As quickly as it comes, it is gone again, and I am once again faced with my own reality. What to do when death encroaches upon me? A fear I don't and can't allow myself to live entirely about but to make sure it is considered in the scheme of life.

The feelings are so intense. They feel like they are flooding all around me; choking me. When someone gets under my skin, it hurts but I mask it with anger and all I want to do is withdraw in order to stop myself from erupting. When I was a child I could run away into the forest through the trees and feel the branches brush past me as I navigated the rabbit trails but in here there is nowhere to go; to escape. I am confined. The worse, part is that if my nature would let me, I would give it up and move on but part of me never wants to; never wants to forget the feelings of days gone past that sit so strongly within me. So, for now, I am forced to contain these and venture inwardly. Not my strong suit. Soon enough they will subside, and I will once again be thrown into my depression. There I will never forget.

I dreamt about being with Rose again. It was so intensely vivid that I awoke aroused, which brought about a sense of guilt and sadness which was soon to be extinguished when I could hear the men speaking outside. The scouts and warriors were heading out for a hunt today. They were in dire need of some meat and the flora had just begun to flower, a sign that there would be plenty of wild beasts about. It would take them the whole day which meant that the camp would be at its weakest, pity I was too, or I could have planned an escape but today I would be content with being let out as Kemp decided that it was time for me to get some exercise.

As I stepped out the sun penetrated my eyes, blurring my vision slightly as they adjusted to its glare. My skin felt warm and I stopped for a minute to take in the moment. With new insight my body jumped to life and fairly easily adjusted to the running; my wobbly legs became more stable as I followed my captor through the open spaces of the fortress. "Follow me." Would be the only commandment I would hear and of course, I copied his movements carefully so as not to be hung by the chain. Over, under, crawling, jumping. Anything to break the monotony of being locked in that cage for hours on end. Plus, I continue to grow stronger and more agile if I put my mind to it. The length of time was short though, before my leg muscles began to burn with intensity but I ignored them and pushed through the pain barrier. I didn't know the time that I would be allowed out again and nature was so rich and vibrant; aesthetically pleasing to my eyes. As my adrenaline kicked in further, I felt a rush of joy flow through me, not unlike a sense of freedom and once again I felt passion. It was something about nature that not only challenged my senses but brought me to life. We sat and stretched out, I remembered the ritual from before and soon felt the burning in my legs subside.

The next few days were followed with the same routine. I could feel myself getting stronger every day and grew anxious for more. And with each session, they became more challenging and I became insatiable. By the third week, our camp was set to move on as we had more than an ample supply from this hunting ground and had already stayed still for too long. I had overheard Kemp talking about the scouts having found a new spot no more than two days walk from this site and they had left some behind to continue observations of the surrounding areas. By now my mental map was growing and I had a pretty good knowledge base of this terrain. Valleys, creeks, mountains, some of them still tripped me up but it took me only a moment to reconstruct the visuals in my mind. A gift from my father who was an excellent orienteer; who would draw in the sand, always showing Chase and me alternative routes both home and around the forest. In doing this we learnt to track quite easily, a necessary skill for our existence today. Chase obviously was a natural as well which is one of the main reasons, he is an excellent scout today.

We walked east until the sun went down on the second day and finally, we had made our new campsite. From what I could see it was three valleys over and in very dense bushland. No Settlers in sight and no sign of nomad tracks anywhere, which meant that we were more than likely alone. I was put to work with the other 'slaves' and was busy setting up a structure on the north side and I noticed that the Razor's ranks were depleted. There must be a lot of them out scouting.

Soon enough, I was reallocated to cook and with a few others we were setting up a fire and roasting last week's kill, wild boar. With the addition of a few of the wild herbs growing around, they were soon roasting on a spit. It must have been the smell because soon enough most of the camp was encircled in the opening near the fire pit and the evening had kicked off with some drumming and dancing. I sat back and watched as a group of them, seemingly careless, skipped about scuffling the dirt as they twirled. I couldn't help but think to myself that in a different situation, I could have actually enjoyed this. At least I was out of the hut and allowed to actually fill my days with something constructive. Soon my eye caught a glimpse of the embers dancing in the fire and I was transcended to my childhood, caught up in its memories of laughter and dancing with my own father by the fire. It seemed like a lifetime ago now, but I still could not help but allow myself to be engulfed in it.

It was the dark of early morning when I heard the distant gunshots ring out. The Razors shifted mindsets and soon through the shouting of commands, battalions were formed. A scouting group had happened upon a Theodoris army who were shacked up in an underground bunker not even a kilometre away. The scout was busy relaying to Kemp what they had encountered. The Theodoris must have been extremely careful to cover their tracks as even our best had no idea that they were even there. It wasn't long before the gunshots got closer to our campsite but with the dense bushland it was hard to know which way the sound was coming from. All I knew was that it was getting louder and more frequent. Leaders filled the tent and as quick as they had come, they were gone. The idea was to surround the enemy and to flank them from all sides. But there were so many variables that Kemp gave a kill-on-sight demand rather than worrying about hostages. It must have been a big camp. From inside of the tent I could hear the gunfire moving from a high intensity to slower caps as the morning sun broke through the darkness. What that meant I did not know but I was sure to find out soon enough.

When the gunfire stilled, I waited and within the hour could hear muffled voices through the trees around me, and then silence filled the air. It was hard to read but I definitely knew something was up, Razors were never quiet when in victory so what was I to expect? Maybe both sides had gone quiet in the thick of the bushland, whatever the case it was doing my head in; I just wanted to know what was going on. Leaving one hell for another was not my ideal situation and being locked in the cage didn't help. I stared intently out of the tent's opening until I was startled by a shadow on the ground. By now I could hear my heart beating and my eyes were wide. "Charlie?" I whispered, shocked. It was one of the other slaves. "How did you get free?"

"Never mind that," he dismissed and with an axe in tow he moved closer. "Stand back," and with that, he thrust the axe onto the padlock freeing me from my cage. "We need to move quickly," he assured. There are a few of us on the outskirts but I fear we haven't much time. I followed willingly and within moments we had snuck around the sentry and we were absorbed by the bushland surrounding the camp. It wasn't long before we found some really dense lantana, around a mile away and slid under it to hide for nightfall. It was too dangerous to travel during the day and with two enemies shooting at will we couldn't risk getting caught, or worse shot. Every now and then we could hear footsteps, but it was too difficult to see who they belonged to and that was really our only saving grace. To be honest I didn't really care either as long as we could get away from this god-awful camp.

As the sun set, we got ready to move. The plan was unclear, but the idea was to get as far away as possible and to obviously not get caught. We slid out from our hiding place and were soon trekking almost stealth-like away from the camp. We were extremely lucky not to come across anyone but were wary to not speak until we were at least ten miles out. It was dark and dense but that's the way I liked it; harder to track and easier to escape. We came across a creek another few miles out and tried to mask our tracks by walking through the water and along the shallows until we were high up in the mountains. The mist was thick up there and it was freezing but walking kept me warm. We ventured around the middle of the mountain and continued along a few ridges before finding a dense space to hide and regroup. It was getting close to daylight by now anyway.

There were nine of us. Charlie, Ben, Jack, Simone, Taylor, Lindy, Kendall, Tom and myself. Charlie spoke first. "We haven't seen anyone yet, so I reckon we keep moving but just be cautious; stick to the dense stuff."

"Do you think it's a good idea to move during the day?" Taylor broke in.

"Well, if we don't, we risk the chance of the scouts finding our scent. The river can only protect us so much."

"That's only if there are any left."

"True, but do we really want to risk it?"

I silently agreed with Charlie, anything to get as far away from Kemp as possible. Together, we decided to keep moving throughout the day to put as much distance between us and the camp.

It was slow though and we were extremely jumpy and not without cause. It wasn't long before we heard rustling in the bushes ahead and like ghosts one by one, we moved behind tall primaeval trees, under thick bushes, and through verdant tangled lantana. I never thought that I would be so happy to see large amounts of that prickly bush. There were many false alarms with rabbits or kangaroos being the culprits. By the time the sun was high in the sky, we were on the cusp of the mountain overlooking a vast valley. A pool of water from a long-forgotten trickle of a waterfall lay before us so we decided to rest nearby and renew some strength.

Simone and Tom had their feet in the water, and we drank as much as our bellies would allow. Even though the flora had just begun to erupt it was still hot and in the scheme of things it was only going to get hotter as the seasons moved ahead.

My feet were aching, but I was anxious to move on. Lindy, a petite girl of about 17 was sitting with me. I remember her from the gathering group. Anything that needed to be collected, that was her job. "Do you think we will actually make it? I mean get away from the scouts?" she asked me warily.

I really didn't know whether we would or not because of their skill but I lied and said, "Of course we will. We've covered our tracks really well so there's no way that they can find us," I added, "but just to be sure we should definitely keep moving and the sooner the better." Charlie must have been thinking the same because before I knew it Simone and Tom were out of the water and we were on our way into the valley below.

Amongst the forest, I found a wild raspberry bush and we ate and filled our pockets for the trek into the valley. It was hard to work out which way we were heading but I think we were continuing southeast, as far as I could tell from the sun. As night fell, we were deep into the valley and had found some dense bushes to hide in. I was out of berries at this point, but it was nice to be free, out in the open, away from Kemp and the Razors. I found a space in the scrub above and looked up into the night sky. It was clear and the stars were out. They lit up the sky like embers in the dark. It was beautiful and I felt a sense of calm fall over me. It was at this point that I knew we were in the clear, it was just a sense, but I was happy to go with that.

Before I knew it, the sun had awoken me, and it was morning. The others were already awake, and I couldn't believe that I had slept. Exhaustion? Whatever the case, I was up, and we were walking within minutes. This time we changed course and followed the contours of the valley and ambled up the next mountain, much higher than the last. We needed to find another water supply and some provisions before fatigue set in. It was lucky that raspberries grew wild in this country, so it wasn't far before we found another bush full to the brim. "Nothing like being a vegetarian," Kendall remarked, and I smiled in response, my mouth filled with berries. The mountain was unforgiving, but we pushed through helping each other as we climbed walls of rocks and toed the edges of cliffs. We reached the top of the mountain by nightfall and found a small spring to drink from. There was a clearing off to one side where we could see out, but we would have to wait until morning to catch our bearings and see what was beyond. Again, I slept soundly, fatigued from the day's climb.

Chapter 10

I awoke first the next day and made my way over to the edge of the mountain. From there you could see for miles around. The bellbirds were singing, and butterflies fluttered playfully nearby. I sat on a rock and for a long time, I surveyed the area, committing as much to memory as I could. Most of it was heading south-east and as I turned to look more towards the east something caught my attention. In the distance I could see a tower, and beyond that what looked like a town. We needed provisions, canisters for water, bags to carry food in and weapons, whatever we could find to keep ourselves alive. But was it worth the risk? It would almost be certainly teeming with Theodoris soldiers. It was then I heard a crack and turned swiftly, "Shit. You scared the life out of me." It was Charlie.

"Sorry. I didn't think to say something." I showed him the town in the distance, and we talked for a while before we were joined by the others. "What do you think about going into town to get some supplies? It's got to be no more than a day's walk. Plus, the Razors won't go anywhere near there." The group was split, but in the end, we were becoming less wary of the Razors and more set on figuring out how to survive on our own and this was one way to enhance our chances of survival. "I don't mind going in with someone to scout if others want to set up a small camp out of town?"

Tom jumped in. "I think it would be better to go in smaller groups then we can see who's about and where to get some provisions. I'll go with Oda." It was settled. Tom and I would scout the place tonight and the others would set up camp out of town and find food.

As night fell and we got closer. Tom and I could see a small amount of light coming from within the town and when we reached the outskirts, we could see Theodoris soldiers in uniform manning the tower that I had spotted from the mountaintop. This would be harder than I had initially thought. We worked out some simple hand gestures for stealth and moved towards the buildings surrounded by the forest. It was pretty easy to move around as the soldiers weren't all that on edge. With the large number, they must have been fairly secure for a long time.

We scavenged in some abandoned buildings first and found three backpacks and two canisters, a lighter and a few bits and pieces of scrap metal that we thought might come in handy if we needed to use them as a weapon. In the next building over there were what looked like five soldiers playing cards in the kitchen, so we snuck in through an open back window and Jackpot, we found a pocketknife, a few more canisters and full packs of gear. No guns but that was to be expected. I thought to get those we were going to have to knock out a few guards.

After surveying the area, we moved back to where Charlie had said the camp would be. It was pitch black at this point as some clouds had come over and we were right on top of them before knowing it. Using the lighter I rifled through the packs and found some new clothes, belts, and rations of food, one pack even had a cooker in it. The best thing was that it was all Theodorisan so Tom and I could get changed and go back in looking like we belong there.

It wasn't long before we were changed and wearing hats walking back into town. Luckily, it was a large settlement as no one really took any notice of us. We could get a better idea of what was really around the place and soon entered a warehouse filled with many usable items. There were even guns in there which really drew us in. The problem was that there were also many more guards in there, so we needed to tread carefully. I had managed to snatch three more pocketknives, rations of food for our camp and two blades before I heard a loud 'Morgan' come from in front of me. Morgan? What the fuck. I looked at Tom's shirt and noticed the name, Kier across his chest. I took a quick look down to find my name, Morgan. I put on my best Theodorisan accent and replied, "Sir." I responded not really knowing what else to say.

"Have you been reassigned to the warehouse? Kier? Well, answer me."

"No, sir. They sent us in to get our weapons and report to the tower for duty."

C'mon, I was thinking, is that really enough to get us out of trouble? "Right. Well, you better get moving. Sergeant O'Hara will give you your assigned weapons so get away from those tables and get over there." Without hesitation and with a 'yes sir' we worked our way over to the sergeant who gave us two AK47s and three rounds of ammo each. Then we were sent packing.

"That was way too close, Tom, let's get the fuck out of here." We headed towards the tower so as not to look conspicuous and then out into the forest to the rest of our crew.

"What the fuck, Oda," Jack was rearing, "I nearly knocked you out. Thought you were one of those Theodoris scum." I laughed.

"That good, huh? And look what we scored."

"Show me that." Upon inspection a loud "fark" came from Jack's mouth, and it was then I knew that we needed to move on and quickly. We trekked further away from town towards the south and by morning had found a place to fill the water canisters and camp for the initial hours of the day. It was there we distributed the first round of gear from the packs. Everyone had a weapon of sorts, rations, a canister and a pack. My biggest find was a compass. Just what I was looking for and there were no objections to me navigating. *Not bad for a couple of nobodies*, I thought to myself. It was clear that we could utilise these outfits but only in the bigger camps where not everybody was known.

My dad had a compass when I was a kid. He would give Chase and me treasure hunts and we would explore new places that he would find around our settlement. That's how I found out where the caves were. Due north east from our campsite but of course, Dad would make it more interesting by sending us on a wild goose chase first. I loved it though. We would find some new plant form and he would hide things he made in the forest in tree stumps and bushes. My favourite finds were always the chess pieces. Having only a pawn to begin with it gave me motivation to want to find the rest so that I could actually learn to play the game and it was his way of making us appreciate the small things; plus, he had to carve the pieces out of wood which was by no means easy as they were extremely intricate. Whatever the motivation as per usual he had taught us yet another extremely valuable skill for life today. I'm beginning to think that he knew all along that we would not only use these skills but need them.

I must have spent at least an hour using the compass marking in my head a map and drawing in the sand which possible ways the Razors would have gone, where we were, where we'd been and where would be the best place to head. "Hey, Oda," a voice broke in. My concentration moved to Charlie.

"I think I've worked it out. Well, some of it anyway."

"What do you mean?" Charlie questioned.

"Well, we've come from over that way, north west. That's around about where we left the Razor camp, and this is where we left town. I'm not sure what's further south of here but if we keep heading this way according to this terrain, we will avoid major cities and maybe happen on a few more smaller towns that we can get more supplies from. Also, if we follow this stream it should lead to a bigger river where we can fish with the line and hooks, we found in the packs. What do you think?"

"You got all of that from a compass? Is it enchanted or something?" I couldn't help but smirk.

"Yeah, something like that."

"Well, we'll put it to the group but I'm in. I could really do with some fresh meat, not that the berries are a bad thing."

It didn't take much convincing, just the mention of fish really got the group on side, so we headed down the stream and as I thought it led through a valley until it branched out into a larger river by the afternoon. We found a spot to fish under the massive open roots of a big willow tree. Tom and Jack dug up some worms and we fished for a couple of hours before sun down. Every time that there was a bite Ben would almost reef the fish right out of the water. But at least they were biting. We got five in total which wasn't much for the nine of us, but I was grateful for anything by this time. Plus, the only additive was the worms and they were very organic. We cooked them on a low fire in some leaves and shared them amongst ourselves. At least we had a spot on the map now where we knew we could come to and find fresh fish. We camped out for the night deciding that we should at least keep a look out, so Kendall and Tom took the first watch. I was on for early morning, so I figured I'd try and get some sleep.

I awoke in a sweat. My dream seemed so damn real that I wasn't really sure if it was a premonition or not. I brushed it off and went to stand watch with Simone. We chatted for what seemed like hours and I found out that Simone worked with the scouts mostly. She would restock them when they came in and in between making sure that all of their packs were sorted she joined provisions and that's how she knew Lindy. It was Lindy who grabbed Simone as soon as the Razors had left camp. She was only tied with rope, so it was easy to get loose and Jack and Tom were already with her when they escaped. Charlie, Kendall and Ben were on the other side of camp and they worked on weapons. Cleaning, restocking the ammo and allocation. Ben picked up Taylor from the tent next to mine and Charlie got me. I think Taylor was one of Smith's girls, but I guess we have some time in finding out for sure. Simone had seen the whole thing from the woodpile right up until we fled. "I wish I had got some more out but it was too risky, and a lot of the larger groups were still guarded by the left-over Razors. Sounds selfish, but at least we got out."

I couldn't help but think the same thing. "You never know. When we get stronger, we may be able to help more people out here. It's the best you could do at the time."

"Yeah, but you know the conditions… It's just… I wish we could have done more."

We sat in silence for a while longer, right up until I spotted him.

He was tall, built, definitely not the type I could take down in a one-on-one. I could count the Theodoris out because he wasn't wearing a uniform, but Razors? I pointed Simone down to him and her eyes widened.

"I'll stay, you go wake the others but tell them to be quiet and quick – he's getting closer. I'll meet you there."

Simone left without a sound and I watched as he moved towards me. On closer look, he was wearing all black and had what looked like a machete in his hand. I crouched down behind a bush to my right so that I was on a slight left of him. He didn't seem to be on any direct route and on closer appearance he didn't look like one of Kemp's scouts but there was no way I was showing myself.

He was within five metres now and heading straight for camp. I needed to think quickly. I had a gun but shooting would be too loud so I would have to wait for him to walk straight past me and even then, I didn't know if he had others. I surveyed the valley and I couldn't see anyone, but Razors are very good at keeping to the shadows. He was right beside the bush when I made the decision, he wasn't changing his route, so I lowered my voice and raised the gun, "Don't move."

Startled, he turned and held the machete firm. Noticing the gun, he softened a little. I forgot I was wearing the uniform. He went to speak, and I silenced him immediately – what if he was to signal any others with him? By now Charles had come from towards the camp and pushed the other gun into his back. "Drop the knife." He demanded. He put the weapon on the ground. "Now push it towards her." He obeyed. Charlie ordered him to the ground and told him to put his hands behind his head. "Jack. Search him." Jack came from seemingly nowhere and he rifled through his pockets finding another smaller knife and a bunch of survival tools. He then picked up the machete. Looking at me now, Charlie mouthed, should we ask him what he's doing here? I took over from there.

"I need you to be quiet and only answer what I ask. Nod if you can do that?" He nodded. "How many are with you?"

"Two."

"Where are they?"

"Back at camp."

"What camp?"

"We are up the valley further. Please…"

"Shhh." I put my finger on the trigger. I thought that I might as well fake it. "Why are you here?"

"I was looking for water. We haven't got much left."

I looked at Charlie. Still not sure of his intent.

"Where are you from?"

"I was at a settlement near the coast and we were raided. We were the only three that made it out alive."

"Where did you get the weapons from?"

"There's a town not far from here. Not many soldiers like you there." That's when I realised of course he's not going to move, that I was wearing a Theodoris uniform.

I motioned to Jack. "Is he clean?" Jack nodded back. "Hold him here." This was directed at Charlie. I looked at Ben and Tom and motioned for them to come with me. "How far is the camp…" There was only one way to find out if he was lying or not. "And which way?" He pointed south east into the valley and said not far. About five minutes' walk. "And weapons?"

"Same as me, knives." I think he figured that I was more interested in checking his story than shooting him.

We moved quickly. It was really easy to track back from his markings. Before we knew it, we had spotted the other two who looked to be packing their gear. "Tom, you flank behind on the left and, Ben, on the right, I'll come from directly in front and get their attention."

Holding the gun tight I approached from the north, "Hands up," I said firmly. They stopped straight away. I was looking at a girl in her late teens and a man in his twenties and they seemed scared. "Please…" she started.

"Wait," I said. "What are you doing here?"

The man cut in. "We have just been camping here. Please we don't want any trouble. We're just about to move on."

I asked the same questions and they were spot on. Either they had their stories set tight or the man with Charles was telling the truth. The girl kept looking up the valley and I noticed her unease.

"Are you going to kill us?" she stammered.

I hadn't thought past questioning and I didn't want to act weak, so I said nothing and motioned them to the ground. Ben and Tom came in from behind and searched them both, again finding two knives and basic gear. At least they had weapons. "How many towns did you pass from the coast?"

He answered, "We passed a lot of towns, over thirty, but we only stopped at one."

If anything, these guys were going to be a really good source of Intel. We met back up with our camp and tied the three of them with some rope from the packs. Tom stayed close with my rifle trained upon the three while the rest of us met a while away. They hadn't seen the others yet, so we kept it that way. "What do you think?" I asked after telling them what the others had said.

Kendall piped up. "We don't know them. What if they're lying and they are really Razors?"

"I think we would have had a lot more scouts on our hands by now, and with these outfits, they would have shot to kill."

Now that I think about it if that was the case, we needed to be more careful.

"Then these guys are who they say they are; escapees like us?" Taylor remarked.

"I suppose so, but what do we do with them now?" This was Lindy now.

And that was the question. What do we do with them?

Me, "I'm not really into hostages so I say we either cut them loose or we join them up."

"What? No way. We don't even know them." Kendall raising her voice started to flail.

"We need numbers, and we still have the element of surprise. They think we're Theodoris." I pulled at my outfit. "They're not going to act out any time soon and look at them. They haven't moved an inch."

Charlie looked at me in agreeance. "Let's put it to a vote. They obviously need help and we keep the weapons. That way we can get to know them better. Okay, raise for yes, lower for no."

Kendall was a definite no, lowered. The rest of the group was cut even so it would be up to Tom. I traded with Tom and waited for an answer. It gave me a chance to find out more from these three and they were open to telling me everything they knew. I was mostly interested in mapping the south to the coast and finding out where the towns were as well as how far it was to the coast. It would be a long trip, but we could make it. There would be more coverage in the rainforest and the coast also meant caves, which is a much better shelter for the hot, rainy months to come. The three of them had been pushing north to escape from their overrun settlement but knowing the Razors they would be well gone by now and the resources would be either depleted or burnt. As long as we didn't venture to the more populated areas, we would be fine. Of course, we would need more supplies, but Tom and I could do that if the need arose.

Charlie came close and whispered in my ear the result.

I aimed the questions at our captives. "So, if you are who you say you are, then are you Wanderers?"

"I guess that's what you could call us. We just want to be free and safe." The first man answered.

"And what is your name?"

"John."

"The girl?"

"Maggie."

"And..."

"Peter."

"What did you do in your camp?"

"I was on weapons, Peter worked with the leaders as a messenger and Maggie, well she was a slave to one of the leaders, Jake."

I asked them to explain a little more about each of their roles to get more insight into how much they knew and whether or not they knew too much. Their answers showed that they were really captives and they showed me the brandings to further prove it. Theirs were on their backs and were a lion inside of a circular shape. I did think maybe they could have been outlawed but with the girl, this would be unlikely. She was way too timid to be a Razor.

"Have you been looking for others?" I asked them.

John answered. "There are no others. There are only Theodoris like you and Razors."

"What if there were others?"

"If there were others, what would you do to join them?"

"Anything. Like I said we just want to be safe and if we could contribute anything, we would but seriously the chances of that happening…"

"Come on out, guys."

Our crew showed themselves and we sat down to talk. We now had three new recruits. I explained how we came upon the uniforms and we shared stories from both sides about the camps that we were in. They had very different ways of doing things but morally both groups seemed to be the same.

I knew it would take Maggie a lot longer to settle in with her history, so I put her with Taylor as she has been through a similar situation. John hung with Charles and me and Tom took on Peter, with their involvement in weapons they had something to talk about immediately. We watched them carefully over the next few days and they seemed to slot into our group effortlessly. Something I wasn't sure about, but they proved us wrong. Maggie turned out to be a really good fisherman and it wasn't long before we packed up camp and started heading towards the closest town that John had mentioned. He said that it was a smaller town so I figured there would be a good start to see what we could find.

It was a day's walk at least before the forest began thinning out and a town appeared. There were no towers, but more soldiers stood guard.

Chapter 11

Tom and I donned a pack and the two rifles and set out towards the camp. I kept going over our names in my head, Kier, Morgan, Keir, Morgan, hoping to alleviate any anxiety that was flowing through my body, but it was temporary as the sooner we got to the town the more hypervigilant I was getting. My brain leapt to life and I screamed inside, get it together, "Hey, you!" Shit, I hadn't even realised how close we were.

"That'll be sergeant to you," I responded without thought.

The man looked me right in the eyes scrutinising my every move, "Well get it together, I'm here from up north to collect the supplies." It was worth a shot. He stared, more intently now. "Do you need me to radio my senior that some guard, Matthews (I read on his to pocket), is holding us up?" He shifted and moved aside.

I was in full stages of panic now. The soldier mumbled something as I wandered past, but I wasn't going to stop and question him, we were in.

The town itself had a wire fence with barbs encasing the tops surrounding it. It was small and there weren't a lot of people settled yet. Tom and I had decided to stay together on this mission just in case of trouble. The others were hidden beyond the outskirts and we had until sundown to return or we were to meet on the next mountain ridge over the next day. Beyond that, we hadn't really made any plans. We passed a few more soldiers who gave us recognising nods which we nodded back, before finalising the scouting of the place. We were near the mess hall across from the supplies house when I pulled Tom up, "Now or never." And he nodded approvingly.

There were two guys standing guard and being the afternoon, a lot of the other soldiers were off in their bunks or preoccupied with some card game I wasn't familiar with. The sounds of yelling and laughter flowed from their tables.

I motioned forward and Tom and I headed for the supply house. We were stopped immediately. "Who are you?"

I waved around my map as if they were orders from my major and spoke firmly. "Like I said to the guys at the gate. We are here to collect supplies for the northern sector. What? Don't you guys communicate around here?" He wasn't convinced. I needed more of a bluff.

"No one enters without orders from Captain Ishma." Ishma? Fuck, now we're done. He told us to stay put and with his gun trained upon us the other soldier, Hamner, was off to find the captain. I could see Tom shuffle in his boots, but I tried to remain as steady as ever. I held the AK closer and tighter just in case the shit was going to hit the fan.

It wasn't long before Hamner returned and he was alone. He whispered something into the other soldier Lye's ear. I could hear my heart stammering, drumming from my body. They've got us now. Hamner turned to us, "Orders you say?"

Firmly I responded, "Yes, we've been through this. Now hurry up we've got a long journey back tonight."

I could feel the droplets of sweat tickling the back of my neck.

"Right, well the captain says there was supposed to be someone coming through in the next couple of days, but you've arrived a little sooner than expected. He said you needed some ammo and guns for reinforcements and a few other pickings. Is that right?"

"That's spot on, but we need to check your supplies unit as well to see if there is anything you need from the base."

He motioned at this point to head on in and they remained guarding the door. Tom and I didn't wait another moment and moved into the house swiftly. We had already discussed what was needed and set about collecting ammunition and four more rifles for our group. We didn't want to take all ten of them in case they grew suspicious. Knives were plenty and we scored a few more uniforms before leaving the unit. It was growing to be late afternoon by this point so we saluted the guards and left them with the thought that there would be more supplies coming soon.

Carrying packs and duffle bags full of our loot we headed back through the forest and up the escarpment to where our camp was. There was no sign of them. We didn't want to call out in case there were soldiers around, so we hid our packs in some nearby scrub and with guns in hand scouted the place. I motioned for Tom to go left and I took right. Looking at the tracks I could see that they were here, and it wasn't long before I was onto their scent. I circled back and found Tom, two is better than one, I thought, just in case we got into any trouble. Time was short when the track went cold, and I heard a loud crack behind me.

I turned, gun in hand ready to fire when Charlie motioned, "It's me. Don't shoot."

"Fuck, Charlie. Way to sneak up on a person with a loaded gun. I nearly shot you."

He calmed down and told me that some scouts came through just after we left so they had to find a new hiding spot. I took a deep breath and called to the others to come out before riddling Charlie with a hundred questions, "How far do you think they got? Which way were they heading?"

It wasn't long before we were back in the bushes where the loot was hidden. Tom piped up, "We got as much as we could without looking suspicious." That's five uniforms and four guns. The others were surprised at what we could get. "We got lucky," I said, "I won't be doing that for a while yet. I was shitting myself. Plus, security is getting tighter."

My head was freaking with the mention of scouts and instead of divvying up the items then and there we kept moving throughout the night further into the mountains and further away from camp. It wouldn't be too long before the real Theodoris would be coming through to pick up their supplies and I didn't want to be anywhere near here when that happened.

It was three days walk before we found a suitable place to camp. Seeing the Theodoris had spooked us all into wanting to get as far away from town as possible. We found a spot with dense bushland, that was mountainous and believe it or not, had rose bushes. It wasn't long before I heard some running water and with a little bit of digging of a tunnel under the rose bushes, we found a hidden cave. It had a small entrance – which was perfect for hiding – and opened up inside with enough room for around 20 people to sleep. Let alone the unexplored crevices further along. We slid along our bellies under the bushes and into the cave, the torches bounced from wall to wall and it wasn't long before we had set up camp and lit a fire. Little did we know at that point that this would become one of our regular hiding spots, far from anything and anyone. We cooked up a few of the tins of food that were left that we had scavenged and shared it amongst the group. There was running water from a small spring – which dripped down into a far pocket in the cave making a small hole before trickling further down the mountain. I was guessing that when the rains came this would be far more useful but gave us all the water we needed for now. Tomorrow we would explore the area further.

First light came and everyone was a little shaky after the long walk, but we needed to find food. Because of their experience, it was decided that Charlie, Ben, Lindy and Simone would don the uniforms and take a rifle each and a knife to set up traps around the area to catch rabbits or any other animals that were in the area. Lindy and Simone had plenty of experience in the hunting and provisioning area and Charlie and Ben worked in the weapons division, so it wasn't long before they were chatting wildly about how to change and hold a weapon and how to make traps using bush materials and bait. Kendall was to wear the other uniform and to take turns staying guard and as a scout with Tom and me in order to keep the camp safe. We weren't sure about the newbies yet so we put them to work on water, wood collection, and any other task we could find at camp. Jack was good with creating structures, so he put them to work securing the place with vines and trenches to keep the water flowing and to also waterproof our sleeping quarters.

The crew had caught three rabbits and a small wild pig the first day, all without making a sound, so things were looking up for all of us. We combined these with berries and native herbs, feasting like kings. The quarters had clay barriers, beds made from nearby bushes, a carefully developed stone fireplace and wood to last for a few days. It seemed to be working. We had created a space to recuperate and catch our bearings.

Every day Kendall and I or Tom and I (whoever wasn't watching base at the time) would go out and survey more of the area around us. We found the river on the map to the South East. Mountains full of berries and herbs surrounding us and valleys with streams and loads of wildlife. We would take string and packs with us to catch fish from the river and streams and got really good at spotting wildlife. Our problem was catching them without making any noise. Jack had devised a solution for this and started making longbows to catch the animals. The problem was – we weren't very good at using them, so a lot of our diet was fish and rabbits for a few weeks. It was over those two weeks we began to settle, and we hadn't seen a single soul. Perhaps we were becoming complacent, but we continued on our way developing our cave into a home away from home. Jack started to teach us how to use the bow and arrows he'd crafted from wood and it wasn't long before we were bagging a much bigger game, albeit a struggle, we started catching bird life and other smaller pigs. On one occasion we captured a kangaroo but that was a rarity.

Chapter 12

Within the month, everyone had been trained on weapons, knives, bows and arrows, in provisions and crafting. There were traps set out everywhere and we were getting regular food at least once a day. We had three times in the day when we would meet up to make sure everyone was safe; sun up, when the sun was high in the sky and sundown when we usually ate a meal together. John, Peter and Maggie slotted right into the group and before we knew it, they were helping with scouting and I began teaching others how to use a compass and to track. This would take a lot longer as I had learnt some of these skills a long time ago.

John and Lindy proved to be good trackers along with Tom, Kendall and I so we would regularly go on scouting missions to see if there were any changes to the bushland that surrounded us. Usually, it would be small animal tracks mostly. It wasn't until a couple of months later that Kendall and I found some unusual tracks down by the river. They were definitely human. My first thought was Razor Scouts, so we hid in the bushes nearby to see if they returned. Sure enough within the hour a small boy and two men appeared. They were fishing down by the river. "Now remember what I said boy, lure them in, show no mercy, you're one of us now." Fuck,

Razors. We crept away back to camp and by sun high we were back at camp debating what had to be done.

Taylor was hugging Maggie in the corner and the rest of us were toing and froing on what was to be done.

"Let's just do them," Ben piped up. "They're obviously on the scout and they wouldn't think twice before killing us." There was a show of approval from the group.

"But what about the young one?" Tom spoke out. "It's not his fault he's been indoctrinated."

This was a dilemma. But as we all knew once this had happened, they would stop at nothing to do what they are told, as a family member was usually held hostage back home.

Lindy was next. "I can't kill a kid, and what about all of the noise? Plus, they'll be trained to the hilt."

"What about if we watch them for a few more days?" It was Peter now. "You know, maybe we could find out if there are any others of them about, where their camp is."

I must admit it wasn't a bad idea, we really weren't sure how many of them there were and whether they would be watching us or not. From then on in we needed to step up our guard.

"Shhhhhhh," came a small voice from the corner. "I can hear something."

Muffled sounds were coming from the bush outside. Fuck! Kendall was out there on watch, had she heard them? It was them – I was more sure of it the closer they came and the more recognisable their voices were.

"There's got to be more people out here." One of the men spoke, more clearly now. "Remember what I said, boy. We need to find more."

Then it became quiet.

Had they spotted us? Heard the water?

It wasn't long before we hear a loud grunt and rustling in the bushes nearby. "I've got her," came ringing through the cave. They've got Kendall.

Immediately, Charlie and Ben had slid under the barrier and were swiftly running in Kendall's direction with Simone and I hot on their tails. More movement could be heard, and we were less careful than usual. We had surrounded them within minutes and were shouting at them to get off her and put their hands up and they were retorting with pleads and large gestures. It wasn't until she arose and ran towards us that we realised that Kendall was nowhere to be seen and that they had in fact wrestled a wild boar to the ground. She was mad too and we jumped aside quickly to let her through. It was then we heard more running and moved to hold the two men and the boy hostage. Ready to shoot we heard a wary voice from the distance, "It's me, don't shoot." Kendall appeared out of the bushes and I couldn't help but hug her as she approached.

"I was heading back to warn you and that's when I heard the scuffle. If the Razors weren't alerted before, they will be now." The taller man started but Ben hushed him quickly with the butt of his gun. We had no choice but to move away from camp and down into the next valley where the interrogations began.

"Where are the scouts?" Charlie began.

"I don't know what you're talking about?" the taller man spoke on behalf of the group.

"Where are the scouts? You were down by the river the other day, were you not?"

"Yes but…"

"Where is your camp?"

"We don't have one." Charlie hit him with the butt of the gun.

"I'll ask you one more time. Where is your camp?"

The taller man took one look at us and said, "We don't have one, we were in a town, months and months ago before it was taken over by you Theodoris and from there on in we've been on the run, fishing and hunting wherever we can." We held up the opinion that we were Theodoris just in case.

I revised my memory, he had clearly said to, "Lure them in." Were they lying to us? The only way to find out was to find some truth serum and make him talk.

"I don't believe you. You are Razors…"

"No please, we're not. We've been on the run and my boy, please…"

That's when I stepped in. "Ben, get some hyoscine from over near the ridge there. We'll boil up some truth serum." It wasn't long before we had them under the serum and in for questioning. It turns out that they were telling the truth and had been on the run for a very long time. We questioned them on their intentions and what they wanted for their small crew. The taller man was named Bill, his shorter companion was Randy and the boy, Hamish. They had managed to move around and camped for a long time. The boy's mother had died during childbirth and there were only three of them. They were tired of moving and were looking for settlements, but they knew that the Razors were becoming more aggressive, so they stayed away from a lot of the bigger ones or were turned away to be left wandering.

We left Ben and Charlie to stand watch while the rest of us went to decide their fate. With a small boy like that and the need for more people in our group, the choice was simple. They were in but not without testing. They would sleep out with the scouts – which were doubled until they had earnt our trust.

Charlie and I were on watch the next day when Bill piped up and asked us about our uniforms. We explained carefully not to give too much away and changed to subject to see what he had done in his past life. It turned out Bill worked in mechanicals and Randy worked on the electric wires. They were part of a settlement way out west which is why they didn't get taken over until much later than us. It had only been a year since the Theodoris had stumbled upon them. Purely because they were half-hidden in an underground town. Bunkers he had called them. I thought it was a little bit weird but realistically that would be the best place to be in a war. Bill explained how they blew up the main piping that enabled better oxygen flow into the place and flushed them out. They were lucky to escape through the underground tunnels that Randy knew so well and only a handful of them got out.

"What happened to the rest of them?"

"They were either captured along the way or split from the larger group. There were a few more in our group who died along the way, disease of sorts, you know."

It would be another few weeks before they were allowed into the campsite and integrated into our new society. Came in handy too, working alongside Jack with the organisation of camp. Hamish was but ten years old, but he seemed older and he pulled his weight as well as the others, trying to prove his worth in the camp. He would collect firewood in mass amounts and started whittling arrows for hunting. He was good at it too. And life went on like this for a while.

It was at this point I was shaken from my memories. Kendall called me from the watch, and it was time to get to know everyone a little more intricately. Jack has a really good sense of humour. He would somehow always see the good in things and create observational jokes from the circumstances. Ben is your strong but quiet type and is excellent at hunting. Maggie even started to come out of her shell and managed to come hunting a few times, although she definitely preferred her fishing, holding the record for the largest fish in our colony. Peter would give her shit and they would always go down to compete because he so badly wanted to hold the record. Bill and Randy started wiring the area with traps for intruders, even devising mechanical things (well beyond my understanding) that would trigger the scout if there was anyone approaching. They used recyclables from the camp and items they foraged in the bush. Brilliant really. Hamish would be in tow still wary of the group and what his role was beyond gathering and whittling. Bill became closer to Kendall and they were always finding ways to 'hang out' together, whether it was scouting, mapping or being on watch. I guess they just couldn't get enough of each other and of course, were not afraid to show it. Taylor and Tom were also hanging out quite a bit, however with Taylor's history she is quite shy, and Tom wasn't pushing anything by any means. He is a patient, nice guy. Simone and Lindy were getting extremely good at provisions and started an apothecary of their own, taking on the role of trappers as well as healers in the group. I taught them as much as I knew, and it was nice to share what each of us knew in our daily catch-ups. And then there is Charlie. Another kettle of fish. He proved to be an excellent huntsman and tracker which really complimented me, so we were spending a lot of time together, mapping out the land. We managed to track back to the town southeast of the main town sign we'd seen and through to the mountains that we were engulfed in. They looked to be called the Courageous Mountains with the highest being Mount Kuruso according to the map.

Chapter 13

Months passed and it was late autumn. We had climbed to the top and looked out beyond the mountains to the abyss beyond. Winter was approaching and that meant snow. So, we needed to pick up the pace on the collection of wildlife and fish during these months. Bill and Randy converted some ground into a fridge using the water from the stream and we started to bury our hunts wrapped in broad leaves for storage during the winter. It was at this time that we realised that we didn't have enough warm clothes. That we would all die of hypothermia before ever making it out of the winter.

Kendall, Charlie and I ventured out the next morning to a nearby small town that was too small to be inhabited by Theodoris. It was there that we would find some clothing for the winter. It would be a day's journey, so we packed light and set off to the township. The farmhouses on the way proved to be full of clothing, with varying sizes, both male and female. We found lots of thermal wear and even managed to filter through a few of the leftover cans left in basements, but they were few and far between. They were out of date years before, but we didn't care, so long as there was food we could store. By the time we had made it into town, it was approaching dark and we knew that we needed to find shelter and shack up soon. There was only one problem, we thought that we were alone.

The first house that we hit is still on the outskirts and close to the bush nearby, so we set up camp there. My feet were aching, so I was happy to be settled. Charlie decided to take watch and Kendall and I decided to sleep in a nearby room. It wasn't until the middle of the night I was awoken by the yelling nearby. Charlie was nowhere to be seen but the adrenaline had kicked in immediately and I was through the door with Kendall hot on my trail. There was a scuffle in the nearby bushes and as we approached carefully, I could begin to make out the voices. "Get on your knees!" came a forceful voice, male. Fark, I mouthed to Kendall and beckoned her forward. I needed to get a good vantage point. Then came a loud crack followed by a moan. It's Charlie, come on, I mouthed again. We were further into the bushes, shielded by them before we saw it. Razors, and plenty of them. I froze but couldn't recognise them in the dark. "Are you alone?" The answer couldn't come quick enough before another crack to the head. "Are you fucking alone?"

The moon came out from behind the clouds and I could see more clearly now. Charlie through blood teeth spat and lied, "Yes." There were four of them. Undoubtedly, they were Razors, but I didn't know which clan they had come from. I whispered to Kendall, "I'll scout around and see if there are any more, you stay put and when you see me come from out of the bushes on the other side, come out blazing on this side too, OK?" She nodded tentatively back.

Thank goodness for the moonlight, I could see into the trees above and crawling along the ground I checked the immediate area. It looked like we were in the clear and had just stumbled upon a small group of scouts. I moved in a full circle before motioning to Kendall and taking my place on the other side. By this time, I could barely see Charlie's face and the Razors were playing with him, kicking him in the ribs and punching his face. I couldn't take it anymore and was about to make my move when Kendall came out from the bushes on the other side, "Found this one too." I must have missed him. Of course, there were more but where was he hiding? "She's a pretty one too." I leant up against a nearby tree and contemplated my next move. If I went out firing, there could be more in the bushes, so I had to come up with a plan. There was a guy close to the edge, one was holding Charlie's weapon, so I moved to target him first. With one swift move, I grabbed his mouth with my left and slit his throat with my right. I didn't have time to think because the others were on me in seconds. I held my ground and pointed the two AKs at them. "Drop the fucking gun," I rustled up as much bravado as I could find to show them, I meant business. They laughed at me but only for a second as I shot one of them right in the head. "Give it to the girl and pass them both over to me, now!" The guy with the gun trained it on Kendall.

"What about I shoot her instead, then I shoot you, and then I shoot him?" The gunshot would have rung out for miles, so I hastened and trained my gun on the shooter. Within moments, I had shot him in cold blood and screamed at Kendall to get the gun. Now we both stood armed and there were only three guys left and they weren't willing to give up. Charlie was on the ground and with one glance I knew what he wanted, we needed to act fast, I looked over at Kendall and we both fired, killing all of them without blinking. It was the only way to get out of this alive.

I grabbed Charlie and we bolted to the packs and back into the bushes and as suspected there were more. The war cry was loud so we needed to tail it further into the mountains, it wouldn't be long before they would catch our trail, our only friend being night. We put distance between us as the cries became softer, but I knew it would be a race against time as the light of day would show our tracks. We decided to lead them east of our base in order to cover our tracks and were careful not to make too much noise but the Razors were the best so we could only hope to find a few creeks or rivers on the way. Luckily, Charlie could still run so we weren't at a disadvantage there, but we knew that we would be in for a long night.

The first creek we found must have been two hills over, so we headed north along its watery banks then we covered our exit tracks so as not to leave a trail. "That should do it," I puffed as Kendall and I moulded the sand and got ready to move northwest back to camp. We picked up the pace and it was mid-morning before we had made it back to the river we fished from. To be sure we made our way through two more creeks and waded through the river before making it back to camp.

"Holy shit." – that was Jack – "What the fuck happened to you?" It was directed at Charlie as we all fell in a heap in the cave.

"Razors," was all Charlie could say.

"Are they here?" Simone cut in. "Are they coming to camp? We need to get everyone in." And with that, she was gone.

"They took Charlie and me in town," Kendall explained, "we thought we were alone, but they must have been scouting for supplies as well. There were more of them, and well, if it wasn't for Oda, who knows what would have happened."

"I think we covered our tracks enough, so they won't know which way to go," I broke in. "We are safe, but just in case we should stay in camp for a while. Just a few people out to gather food but that's all."

I needed a moment, so I volunteered for the first watch.

I had just killed people in cold blood. I knew that it was the right thing to do but somehow it followed me. What was I really capable of? I knew that they were Razors and it was my friends over those murderous souls, but I couldn't stop shaking. The adrenaline was obviously wearing off and reality was sinking in. The scenes kept replaying in my head and I couldn't stop them. The shots, the yells, cutting a man's throat? Gladly, Kendall showed up and sat down beside me. "I just wanted to thank you."

"You would have done the same for me."

We sat in silence, but I was happy to have the company.

It wasn't long before Ben and Lindy came to replace us, and I was once again deep in thought, in the cave. Simone had patched up Charlie and he was sleeping soundly in the corner. At first, I couldn't sleep, every time I closed my eyes the images would come back, haunting me. But my body got the better of me eventually putting me into a deep sleep.

The sun pierced my eyes and I knew it was morning. I didn't remember dreaming that night, it must have been the exhaustion, but the flashbacks were still with me. I needed to shake them and the only way I knew how was to keep myself busy. Simone was heading out to check the traps, so I went with her. Her company would be the best thing for me. The air was already starting to thin and it was getting cooler in the mornings, so I grabbed a jacket with my AK and moved with Simone cautiously just in case they had found our tracks. We needed provisions and I had to be needed at this point it was the only thing I found weirdly enough that could make me worthy again. Not a murderer anymore.

With no sightings of the Razors, we used the time wisely and set about finding other potential places in the mountains. Charlie and Ben moved north, and Kendall and I went west. We hadn't mapped the west end properly yet so I gave the compass to Kendall, it would be good practice, so we took some packs with provisions and we set off in the mid-morning. It wasn't long before Kendall and I approached the topic of the Razors from the day before. I would rather have forgotten it. "I didn't get the chance to talk to you about yesterday, to see if you are alright."

"We really don't need to…" I urged them to discontinue the conversation.

"No really. I couldn't have borne going back… there."

"You would have done the same for me."

"I think I froze when they grabbed me. Are you OK?"

"Yeah, sure. Couldn't be better." I lied. "Just glad we made it back and there weren't any more of them. The situation could have been way worse than it was, you know."

I froze when I saw it and motioned with my pointer for Kendall to hush. To tell you the truth, I was partly glad I didn't have to talk anymore. In front of us was a wild goat and I wasn't ready to pass up the opportunity to snag some dinner for the group. I took out my bow and within seconds had taken the wild beast to the ground. Beside him, I said my usual rant for his soul and thanked him for our food source. In my head, of course, I didn't want to seem crazy, crazier than usual anyway. We found a fallen branch nearby and tied him to it to drain. "We'll swing by on the way back and take him home."

From there the land dipped down into a valley and it was there that we found our water source. I jumped into the stream loving every moment of the cool refreshing water. *What it would have been like to be a kid again*, I thought as my mind went wild thinking of freedom and laughter. Kendall and I swam for a while before heading upstream to a smaller waterfall. The mineral-rich rock wall was unusually steep, so it took us a while to scale it but at the top, there was an abundance of berries for us to collect. It was beyond noon now, so Kendall and I feasted on berries while we followed further upstream.

Something flickered in the corner of my eye. It was bright and it only took a moment for me to pass it. Cautiously, I moved towards it. "Wait here," Gun barrel pointed and my senses heightened it wasn't long before I had reached it. Covered in debris it looked like it hadn't been touched for years. I pulled back the decay and below I found a hatchet. I motioned for Kendall to come closer. "Train your gun into the hole, I'm going to open it." It took brute force to move the wheel holding the hatchet into place but finally, it broke and I opened it further. "Ready?"

"Ready."

I pulled open the lid and instantly fell backwards with the smell of it. "Holy shit," I gagged, "what in the hell is that?"

"Fark, smells like…"

"Death," we voiced in unison.

Chapter 14

I covered my mouth with my scarf and turned on the torch. "I need to check this out." What was I thinking? It wasn't enough that there could have been anything down there. We followed each other down the ladder and into the den below. At first, there was a tunnel, short and dark. The torches let in some light and we ventured further. It wasn't long before it opened up into a massive room. That's when I saw it. In its day it would have been a communal kitchen area. Tables, sink, oven, the whole nine yards. But there in the corner lay two skeletons, partly preserved by the seal. "Yep, dead people." One was holding a gun.

We continued on and there was a bunk room with three more dead people laid out on their beds. It looked to me like they'd been there for a long time. Further along, there was a bathroom. I turned on the tap and it shuddered then moments later fresh water came streaming out. "Jackpot!" I couldn't help myself.

"I wonder what happened here?" Kendall spoke out almost scaring me through the silence.

"I don't know; it doesn't look good. What do you think though? About the place I mean."

Kendall looked at me willingly. "Well, it seems to be what we need. Freshwater, beds even. What more could we ask for?"

The one entrance in and out was what I was afraid of, but I thought we'd run it by the group when we got back. "C'mon, we better get going if we're to make it back before dark." I battened down the hatch and covered it with nearby debris and branches. Stepped out the distance back to the waterfall and we headed back to camp.

We were welcomed with open arms when the group saw the goat and the berries that we had collected from the falls. Lindy took the goat and Jack and she were busy getting it ready for dinner. Charlie and Ben weren't back yet and Simone was on watch, but we told the rest of the group about our find and were met with mixed responses. I could understand, it was eerie that there were bodies still sitting in there. Not soon after we had finished Charlie and Ben had returned with fish and more fresh berries, good for breakfast. They had found a few spots to the north but not enough coverage for the whole group just for scouts and anyone who needed a quick hiding spot. "Grub's up," came a voice from beyond and we all sat down to eat and talk about the newfound places, where they were and how we could use them to our advantage. It was agreed that we would all venture west tomorrow to check out the burrow and Bill and Randy would head north in the afternoon to see what they could rig up to create better hiding spots where Charlie and Ben had located them.

Gunshots spoke to me in my dreams with the faces of the dead passing before me. This is what I dreaded, the nightmares. Kemp was coming for me and everywhere I turned Razors would appear. I kept firing though but the bullets were like ghosts in the dark. But there was no way that they were taking me. I awoke in a sweat. It was still dark, but I couldn't get back to sleep so I went out to join Charlie on watch. "Hey, what are you doing up?"

"Can't sleep."

"Well, pull up a pew. I need some company. Getting bored out here."

"Thanks."

We sat in silence for what seemed like an eternity, with nothing but racing thoughts running through my head.

"Hey, Charlie."

"Yeah."

"What do you reckon about this place we found?"

"It's kind of weird that there were people there."

"Yeah, that's what trips me up too, but to tell you the truth, it looks like they took their own lives. From what I could tell anyway. It looked to me like a family was down there. It may have been even just after the war."

"In that case, no one would know about it. That means it would be secure and safe."

"Yeah, I'm just concerned about the one entrance in and out, but it could be an option?"

The conversation went to old times and Charlie and I both told stories of the old days until the sun came up.

We had fish for breakfast and set out soon after. I warned the crew about the smell and soon enough we were inside the main room. Everyone moved about the separate rooms each in their own conversations. Bill and Randy were busy rattling off their technical jargon and I was nodding unknowingly at what they were saying. Something about power, generators and defensive strategies to keep us safe. I figure as long as they knew what they were talking about, who was I to interfere? We moved the bodies skyward and buried them a fair way off, then sat down to chat near the waterfall. "So, what do you all think?"

It was a mutual yes, it definitely sounded like the better option for now anyway.

The boys were set on working the wires and already we had set up camp in the room. I must admit it felt nice to have a bed for once. It reminded me of my settlement. We set up watch in the trees nearby, the bush was fairly thick so it was hard to see but that meant it would be even harder to see us. The watch had to make sure that the hutch was covered at all times and we set up a false floor covered in foliage for the watch to hide in, just in case. I spent the afternoon down at the waterfall. I had lulled myself into this false sense of security. I really just wanted to feel something again, I don't know, like alive or something. Something as far away from my reality as possible so I lay on the rocks and looked up at the sky. Nothing. And that's the way I liked it. I could feel my heart beat through my chest and it wasn't long before the rhythm had rocked me off to sleep.

Darkness engulfed me and I was confronted with the faces of the lost. I couldn't make them out but there was a looming smell in the air. Like death. Blood. Then something beckoned me awake. Charlie was shaking me. His face was pale. "What's going on? Are you OK?"

"Huh, yeah, I'm OK," I replied yawning as I wiped the sleep from my eyes. "Not much to report on here." I lied.

"Weird, you were moving like a mad woman. If you're OK then, you're up for the watch with Kendall."

I rose from my rocky bed, collected some wild plums from a nearby tree and moved to my position next to Kendall high up in one of the blue gums. It was really beautiful here, but I couldn't help but wonder to think about the last inhabitants. What had really happened to them? It looked like a murder-suicide, but it could easily have been a murder scene. One door in, one door out and with that the first signs of the winter to come fell in snowflakes on my head.

The beauty of winter was that the Theodoris and the Razors would be slower moving, the raiders would be heading further north, and the army would stay closer to town. This meant more time scouting and less time worrying about invaders. My gut feeling was that we could not stay here but somehow, I wanted it to be home. Kendall and I nestled quietly in the tree alone with our thoughts. The time passed quickly and before I knew it, it was nightfall. It was hardest at night on watch. There were noises from nearby animals, leaves falling from trees and of course the waterfall, all accentuated by the clarity of night. At least it kept me out of my head for a while. It wasn't until dawn I saw my first reason for concern. I was scouting further from our area when I noticed fresh footprints in the snow. Beckoning Kendall we pursued them and finally came to the outskirts surrounding a river crossing. There by the river was a small girl, a woman and two men. They were bathing and fishing. I checked over their clothes briefly and noticed that they had no weapons. "What do you think, Kendall?"

"They don't look like Razors, well, I mean the way they're acting," at which point the men started diving and flailing in the water, almost playing, "and they aren't wearing any uniforms."

It was a unique situation, how are they wandering around free? I questioned myself.

We decided to come out of the bushes and show ourselves.

"Hey, you!" Kendall called out.

They immediately froze and one of the men shouted back, "Please, we'll be on our way soon." All of them had their hands raised in the air.

"What are you doing out here?" Kendall again.

"We are on our way through," came the voice from the man, "just trying to find a place to sleep. I have a young child here. We don't want any trouble."

"Where have you come from?" These were all becoming standard questions.

"South, we heard of a settlement up north of here. At least a month's walk. We're hoping they'll let us stay for the winter."

"What sort of work do you do?"

"Me, I'm Joe and I'm, well I was a farmer, my wife Camilla looks after the kids, well kid now, this is Josie. Todd here, he can track really well, and Michael well he can build anything."

Kendall turned to look at me. I raised an eye, they seemed harmless, I mean who would be stupid enough to work their way through these woods without weapons?

I piped up. "How long have you been… out here?"

"A few winters now. We were in a settlement east of here until it got taken over by a Theodoris camp. A lot of us got away, but we are the only ones left in our group. Others were taken by Razors along the way."

Josie was eyeing off my golden necklace, I shifted uncomfortably. I pulled the scarf higher over my neck to hide it. Then I thought for a moment. We could really use those skills in our camp and if they pull their weight, they could help us track food for the winter. It came out briskly, without further thought. "We've got a camp near here. Why don't you come and meet some of our crew?"

"Well, I don't know. I'm really not sure whether to come back with you, with guns and all. I know you're not Razors otherwise, we'd be goners by now, but we've had our measure of bad decisions if you know what I mean?"

"Yeah, us too. It's just with a family and there are lots more Razor camps north of here. Do you really want to risk that? Your choice but."

He ummed and ahhed until finally, the group came to a decision. It was a big move on my behalf too, letting more in but I knew we'd need them. Especially if we were to survive the winter.

Looking timidly around, defeated, he spoke, "OK. Well, we've been travelling a while now, and we could use some rest."

"The only thing is you'll need to contribute, you know, with hunting and gathering supplies and the like."

"Yeah, well, we can do that."

Within the next beat, we were off back to camp. I pulled up a while out and called to Jack who I could see was nervously looking on. "Jack, get the crew, I want you to meet some people." There were many different responses from the group, and I knew that this one would be on me, but I had a good feeling about it all. We didn't take them to our bunker but rather kept them at a distance until we had questioned them further with hyoscine.

Lunch was cooked so we all sat down to hear about stories from the East. I was hoping to get time with Todd alone so that I could start to track to the east as well. See if there were any good hiding spots, they had found to further our repertoire.

By the afternoon, we had put everyone to work and I got my wish, time with Todd. I laced his drink with hyocine and I questioned him intently about places we could use as hiding spaces. I found out that there were at least two spots that were worth a look. He proved to be excellent with the compass and a really good tracker. By the afternoon, we had hunted a dozen rabbits and a deer. It was all I could do to keep myself feeling alive at this point. I must admit the new people were a welcomed change as I was beginning to concede to the cabin fever and the monotony of the routine of what was now to be my new life.

It was Charlie who approached me. "Are we inviting anyone now?"

"Huh." I was woken from my dreams of the East. "C'mon Charlie, seriously, I checked them out first. Plus, I had a really good gut feeling about it. We need more people to hunt and gather provisions."

"It doesn't matter, we don't know these people, you are putting us all at risk."

I must admit it hadn't really entered my mind at the time. "Charlie, it's on me then, isn't it?"

Charlie motioned to push further but I was already into the bushland and off to my post for the afternoon. It would have fallen on deaf ears anyway. It was something in the little girl's eyes that prompted me, and nothing could change that fact. Maybe she reminded me of home back in the settlement, maybe she reminded me of me.

The afternoon was mundane. I sat in my usual tree for hours but this time I peeked back through the trees to the camp and watched Josie playing with her mother. And at that moment, I started to sob. Deep heart-wrenching sobs. I kept trying to choke back the tears but the abys kept pushing for more until the gentle stream became a rushing river and I was gasping for breath. I couldn't help but think about my own childhood and like a rush it all came back. I would give anything to have had just one more moment with my own mother. Anger overcame me and I brushed back the tears. It was then I heard it. A small but startling rushing of bushes. Alarmed and confused I thought – more than one. That is way bigger than a deer.

Chapter 15

Then it clicked Todd had gone tracking, "Run!" I let off two warning shots, but it wasn't enough. They were upon us in moments. There were at least thirty of them charging our camp. I could hear screaming and rifles going off one after the other, and I was overcome.

They dragged us out into a nearby clearing. Having taken our weapons, they were licking their lips with insatiable lust. Then it hit me. Fuck, this was me. They were Razors and very good at hiding it. I had become one of those, people who are blinded by seeming innocence and now my friends would pay the price.

It wasn't long before they had segregated us, and an unusually large man was standing guard over Kendall and me. It was then that I noticed that not all of us were there. Jack, Tom and Charlie were missing. There was a slightly different air about these Razors, they didn't strip us there but rather watched us. I felt uncomfortable at the silence that engulfed us all. It did nothing to prepare us for what was to happen next. A call went out and it would be a while longer before a large group of men came to the site. They had us completely surrounded and started by taking Taylor, Simone and Lindy first in the line. Next were the boys present then at the rear were I, Kendall and Maggie. Our traitors had taken up the rear behind me and were discussing where the open camp was before a few of them moved towards it. It wasn't long before the big man spoke with them as well and approached me daringly. He forced my scarf from me and smiled at me maliciously. Anger rose within me and I spat on him. He pushed me to the ground with ease and there laying in the dust I contemplated our fate.

It wasn't long before he picked me back up and we were dragged due north across the countryside. The Razors here didn't bother with finding our camp rather they urged us on. I was still confused but I knew they were Razors because who else would know about the gold? It would be days without rest before we would meet our fate.

The camp was small, lesser than what I was used to but there were enough to overpower our minor group. The scouts called through the trees and within moments there was a hell of a lot more Razors surrounding us. Wolf whistling, snarling, cussing, but in reassurance, the only ones touching us were the ones urging us forward. We were assembled in the middle of camp and it wasn't long before the stares moved to me and there was whispering all around me. It seemed they'd all known.

A man came forward and motioned us to the ground, "Lay forward, on your bellies." I didn't move but something hard pushed into my back. It wasn't long before I was lying in the dust again. "This is her; the one Kemp has been looking for."

Looking up I could see the chief's eyes widen in what looked like luck and fear embraced as one.

"Are you certain?"

"She has the mark."

He pulled at my collar and the chief stepped forward.

"Take her to my tent."

I tried to fight but it was no use he was much stronger than me and before long I was chained inside a small tent, confined to looking at the canvas only to hear what was happening outside. And there was lots of commotion now. Screaming, yelling, laughing, loud thumps and it was all my fault.

Night fell and the screams became nothing but etchings in my mind. I couldn't sleep so I just sat there staring into the hole that was the door of the tent. We didn't have a chance. I didn't even give our group a chance. All that work to be what? Back in the clutches of the Razors, back to where I started. In chains. The chieftain came in and he had Kendall with him. I knew this was going to be a long night. "Not her," I compelled, "take me instead." But he wasn't interested so I was destined to hear Kendall's protests and the chief's groans all night. I replayed the day over and over in my head and succumbed to the guilt that was encompassing me presently. It was consolidated by my grief for Kendall and the others, who were reaping my mistakes of mine.

Days went by and I was stuck. Unable to move from the tent and under the watchful eye of Razors. It was a week later before I heard his voice. I'd know it from a mile away. It was Kemp. He was here. My heart started pounding and I suddenly had a problem with my breathing, that is not being able to breathe. I found myself gasping and then as the shadow engulfed the tent I froze completely. I completely flipped out. In an instant, I was in the corner as far away from him as humanly possible. It had been months since I had seen him, but he hadn't changed a bit, as my focus changed, and the sunlight's glare had passed I could now see his face. A wry smile across it. He moved towards me and I cowered. Lunging he struck me, his face changing from a smile to a psychopathic glaze. Coveting me. He picked me up by the throat, his hugeness engulfed me, and he pulled me against his body. He had grown, filled out and his penis was hard against me. I couldn't help but writhe, and within seconds I had vomited all over him. He laughed maniacally, dropped me to the ground and left.

The chief came in with two men and pulled me from the tent. I went all floppy and then in between being dragged I tried to pull against them. In an automated response, I started to cry, scream and fight all at once. It's like my body jolted into gear and I was moving again. The blood was pumping, and I was fierce. But I couldn't get free. Outside the glare hit me again and for a moment, I was blinded, but it didn't stop my olfactory sense from taking over. Blood, I could smell blood and it wasn't long before my sight came back and I saw for the first time, hanging in the trees. The men. I couldn't help but scream.

"No, you fuckers, you fuckers. Have you no conscience?" I scrawled across to the other end and the women were naked and chained to a pole. I yelled out to them. "I'm sorry. I'm sorry." And then everything went black.

I woke in the heat sweating profusely. I was out in the open. Strapped to a tree. All I knew was that I was back in my jail. Back with the demon.

The camp was rising and there was a small congregation of people I recognised watching me as they went about their morning chores. By now I was trying to struggle free, but it was to no avail. I was trapped. Again. I couldn't help but begin to shake as his voice neared. By the time he was standing in front of me, I was in a full-blown panic attack. Kemp grabbed me and his thugs untied me. Struggling, I was dragged all the way to what his tent was now. The room opened up into a small space with two women sitting quietly on the wooden framed, hurriedly created bed. *They must be his new girls*, I thought to myself, and once again kicked at him. It was no use he moved quickly and laughed at my feeble attempt. He pushed me onto the bed face first and whispered in my ear for me to spread my legs. There was no way that I was going to do anything that he asked so I pushed my knees together in a rage. "Fuck you."

He grabbed me tighter and through gritted teeth, he spoke, more like a command this time, "Do what I say. Spread them." Then he forced me taking my right and tying them to the wood beneath the bed. He did the same with the other. He pulled me back by my hair and ran his tongue down my neck. I shuddered and once again the vomit threatened. He tied my hands above me and commanded the girls to strip. This constant confusion had taken over my emotions and I found myself second-guessing the anger and the fear. It wasn't long before I knew his intentions. He told the girls to kiss and then he lowered his arm from the bed in front of me. With one brisk force, he hit me right in the ribs. It was enough to double me over so that I was putting tension on the rope above. He hit again from the other side winding me. As I gasped for air, he removed his shirt and joined in with the girls behind him. I looked away. I couldn't watch this. With my eyes closed tight, I heard every moan and gasp. It made me sick at the thought of it. They came together in one loud grunt and then it was quiet. I was thankful for the peace and curious as to why the fuck I was here. Like always, Kemp was playing with me. He liked to make me feel inferior to him and I guess in order to show how powerful he was he had to make me submit and I wasn't ready to do that yet. I scowled directly at him in protest and it wasn't long before he had me back in my corner tied and alone. It was only a short time but being here I felt the claustrophobia gaining on me. I passed out.

All I could do from going crazy was to think of ways to get out. To escape. I tried the ropes and the burns were there as reminders of my failure. Most of all, the fear of his return made me so anxious every moment of every day that I thought that I was having multiple heart attacks or in the quiet moments heart palpitations. One of the hardest things was that I was alone with my thoughts. The grief came rushing in. The faces of my friends hanging from the trees, naked for all the Razor camp to see. How could I have been so stupid? But I couldn't feel sorry for myself. It was them who took the fall for me. I was supposed to look after them to be smarter, but I wasn't, I had lulled myself into this false sense of security. I thought we were safe. That we were far from the dangers imposed upon us by the Razors. But I now knew that this was not the case. That they are everywhere and there was nothing that would stop them from capturing more out of pure greed. They would use any means necessary and I needed to be smarter.

Kemp entered, slowly and seductively. The only thing was that I wasn't interested. "Good to see you again, Oda." The feeling was not mutual. He poured himself a drink and rested on the bed. "You will never get away from me," he snarled almost hurtfully. "I have eyes and ears everywhere. I own you."

"No, you fucken don't. Nobody owns me, nobody. You are nothing to me," – the words escaped more easily now – "you are just a psychopath with a fucked-up obsession. You all are. There is something wrong with you."

He laughed. "You were born a Razor so get off your high horse and rather than opposing me accept your destiny, accept who you are."

Who was I? I had no idea who I was. This product of my circumstances was all that I could associate with. I didn't want to be who he said I was but to a certain degree, I was born into it, but is that what defines me? Or can I create who I want to be? Escape from my past and embrace my future. My future. It's looking bleak but I need to remain true to the hope in my heart. Hope to get out of here, to live free and without oppression. Isn't that all anyone wants? I guess not. Where there are people who want to control there will always be people who want to be controlled, but then there's the rest of us.

"I am not who you say I am. All I want is to be free."

"You will be. If you just accept who you are and live with me. You can have anything you want. As long as you submit."

Submission just wasn't in my blood. I wouldn't, I couldn't, that's not who I am. And is that really who he was or was this again another product of circumstance, of social conditioning of life and choice?

"I can't. It's not in my nature. I will not submit to you."

"You will. It's just a matter of how."

He came close, picking me up under the shoulders and turned me to face the tent. Behind me, he started pulling me towards him and he kissed my neck, running his hands down my torso to my groin. I couldn't help but feel guilty as my body became aroused. It was like the whole world wanted me to feel it. It had been a while. He untied my hands and pulled them behind my back. His strength holding me with one hand. The other caressing my lower torso moving towards my breasts. My body was betraying me. I could feel my nipples harden underneath my shirt. It wasn't long before he had my shirt off and laid me on the bed. I couldn't move, he had me pinned. I could feel him, stiff, and his muscles rippled on top of me. It was a hateful scene, but I couldn't help but feel provoked. My mind drifted to better places. To lakes and the bush and to freedom. I barely noticed my trousers being removed and was all but surprised to feel him inside me. Moving faster and faster, I felt alive and shameful all at the same time. I could hear myself and it was surreal, almost like it was an out-of-body experience. My body was encapsulated and my mind distant. But, nonetheless, I came, moments later he came too. Ashamed, I was back in ropes before I knew it. More confused than ever.

The one thing it gave me was a new obsession – to escape. And soon.

Kemp and I slept together for days and I went to another place every time. It was hard enough to try and fight so eventually I just gave in. I didn't submit, I just couldn't be bothered spending the energy when I could be thinking of ways to escape. I fantasized every day and I wished that he would just let me go. We talked more, butting heads with every philosophy he tried to spin. In his efforts to try and convince me to stay, he was pushing me further away.

He was in one of his rare playful moods and with guards at the post he let me run free. I moved into the corner in an attempt to escape but in doing so I had also trapped myself.

An inferno rushed over me and I was fighting to be free, free from his control, free of this life, free of this world. I punched and scratched but again it only made Kemp more amused and of course me fuller of retribution. But it was no use – he was too strong for me. He wrestled me onto the bed and for a moment he held me there looking into my stubborn eyes. I defiantly looked back searching for ways to escape. To no avail, he pulled up my shirt and began caressing my abdomen, down to my hips, manoeuvring his tongue, making my skin prickle. Soon he was upon me again teasing each nipple to no end. I wasn't giving up this time – I pushed hard against him. Almost putting him off balance. Noticing, he pushed back harder pushing me further into the makeshift bed. Then he continued to remove my shirt and used his fingers to softly play with my neck, his tongue embracing my ear lobes. I was disgusted and not afraid to show it. This time my body would not betray me. I stood firm on this notion. In one swift movement, he had me on my front hands cupping my breasts, kissing my back ever so gently. He pulled my ass close to his groin, holding me in this position whilst he fondled my breasts. I could feel myself getting wet beneath him. In one swift move, he had removed my pants and I was seated, leaning back on top of him. He had one arm tightly around my waist and the other on my nipples pulling them together tightly. His tongue was searching my neck and I was struggling beneath him. I had gotten stronger from being out in the wild, but I was still no match for him. It wasn't long before the hand holding my waist moved to my hip and he tickled me in its crevice. I moved quickly, startled. Slowly, he moved further down until he finally rested cupping my vulva, one finger poised at the entrance to my vagina. I could feel him smile as he felt the wetness below. Slowly, he started flicking his finger at the entrance making me both cringe and beg. "Please?" I said not knowing whether it was to stop or to enter in. My question was answered with a quick movement of his thumb on my clitoris. He stroked, gently at first but more convincingly as the night went on, still holding me tight by my breasts. It wasn't long before I started to lose control, I started to arch my back and he took advantage of that slipping a finger inside. But I was not satisfied, I wanted more. I arched further and he pulled me closer, inserting another finger. It wasn't long before he found my G-spot and I was encapsulated in both pleasure and pain. My head began to heat up and I was losing control. I had stopped fighting long ago and he had taken advantage of that, pulling my hips into his groin. His hardness against me. I was coming. I let out a soft gasp and just as I was heating up, he pulled me onto him dragging my hips over his as I faced away from his face. He yanked me harder and I couldn't help but push with him. Kemp started to tremble, and I was already beginning to come, the breadth of what lay beneath covering his body. I quickened and electricity started running through my body. My breasts thrashed and swelled with every move. He quickened and in one last movement, we came together. I lay there next to him, unable to move, exhausted. But it wouldn't be long before I would get my energy back. When I did, he rushed to tie me up, stumbling, he left.

In his haste it was loose, and I was going to take advantage of that. I slipped the rope from my hands and crept up the side of the tent to the opening. Careful not to make a sound, I snuck up behind the watch and choked him out making a run for it. Running to the tree line. I had no idea where I was, so I tried to run to the densest part of the bush. Allowing it to swallow me whole. It was then that the calls went out.

Chapter 16

The scouts had spotted me, but I wasn't going back. There was no way. I ran until my heart gave in, scratched up and bleeding I ended up in the midst of thick lantana and there I stayed watching the footsteps run past and the calling of the Razors through the trees. Like a stunned rabbit, I froze and didn't move. There was no way that I was going back.

It would be days before I would move. I just had to be sure. Razors inspected the lantana but not close enough to see me through its thicket. I lay silent until the cries had gone, and scouts were becoming scarcer.

Rolling out from my hiding spot, I knew that it was time for me to venture south again. I had a plan to go to our original hiding place behind the rose bushes. Mountain after mountain flew past each looking the same as the last. I snacked on bush plums and berries – whatever I could find. It would not be long before I got there but I was not alone.

It seems that Kendall and Simone had broken free from the Razor camp as well and we met with a warm embrace. "I'm so sorry." The words continued to echo from my mouth. But I knew nothing could right the wrongs that I had committed.

"It was horrible," Simone remarked, "I can't even put words to what they did to us. Kendall and I got out but the rest of them. They were chained. I couldn't help them."

"It's OK." Was all I could bring myself to say as the guilt rose within me. It was all my fault of course. But right now, it wasn't about me.

We sat in silence for what seemed like an eternity and soon I went to remove the footsteps in the snow which would direct anyone to our hideout. Then I remembered – the boys. It wasn't safe to venture that way, so we decided to stay put.

Inside the cave, there were loads of supplies still there from before the move to the bunker and I remembered that outside there was a plethora of animals buried beneath the snow. So, we knew that we wouldn't starve in the next while anyway. There was also an AK that we left behind just in case so at least I had the means to catch food although we were really low on ammo. So, it would be back to creating a bow and arrow and hoping for the best in the worst season for hunting.

The world around us was bleak but that wasn't about to stop us from regaining our happiness. It had always been cruelling for us. We had no luck and had lost the ability to know which direction was right. So, we just existed until it was well into spring and the world had come alive again. It would take that long for me to regain confidence in myself after leading so many of us to certain death. After a few weeks, I went to the bunker and found the boys still holed up.

A shot rang out as I opened the bunker.

"It's me, Oda."

"What the fuck happened?" Charlie beckoned.

"We were taken. You were right. They were Razors and very good. Everyone is either dead or taken. Only Kendall and Simone escaped and are waiting for me to return at the rose bushes."

"Jack was quick enough to get back into the bunker and warn us. We haven't been anywhere in weeks."

"It's not safe here. C'mon, let's go."

We filled our duffle bags with supplies and headed back to the others.

The day had led me to the creek, and I was bathing when I heard a snap in the woods nearby. Immediately I submerged and through the reeds, I could see them. They were Razors, the only thought in my head. My heart skipped a beat and I froze. They were heading straight for me. I managed to unstiffen myself and moved even closer to the dense reeds. By now they were right on top of me.

"C'mon, Angent, I just need some water and then we'll keep looking."

"Not the right timing, we're on patrol," an unfamiliar voice returned.

"Fuck this, I'm always patrolling and looking around, we aren't going to find anything out here. The scrub is too dense."

I was aware of my nakedness now and flinched further as they moved towards my exposed clothes.

"Monica, keep to the mission. This is why I hate scouting with you. You're so easily distracted. We need to move now."

I waited until they had followed the creek north and were out of sight before I allowed myself to unravel, my body shivering in the cool waters. Quickly, I got dressed and alerted the others.

"We are not alone." I motioned to the group.

Shock hit their faces as we moved to cover our tracks and put the fire out.

"Who was it?" Kendall spoke up cautiously.

"I don't know, Razors? Scouts? They seemed quite relaxed in their scouting."

Simone piped up, "It doesn't matter who they were, I don't want anything to do with outsiders."

You could tell the last camp had taken its toll on her, on all of us. Everyone was an enemy now and we needed to be extra careful not to give up our only hiding spot.

I was happy at least that I still had company and it was no time at all before we were back into the same routine. There were groups that came through both Theodoris and Razors but most of them kept out of the dense forest mirroring the lakes and nearby streams. I could see them from my gum tree from time to time, but no one ever came close to our camp. I took the time to thank whoever that I escaped quickly from Kemp's grasp and was able to find my way back without complication. Of course, it was meant to be and now there was no way I was going back. No way in hell.

It was back to hunting for us and very carefully we trod. There were too many people about these days not to be careful, but we were running out of food and the plums and berries we'd scavenged all but a few in the area. It was time to go further afield. We took the guns we had left, some knives and the bow and arrows scavenged from the bunker and headed off to hunt. It was a long time before we found the game, but it was a good time to catch up on how Simone and Kendall had escaped. Of course, they were strong, to say the least, but I didn't realise how cunning they could be. Both of them had devised a plan whereby they needed to go to the toilet and with one guard on watch, they were able to take him out and get away but not without the Razors chasing them. It was luck really that they had hidden amongst a tree's open trunk and the Razors couldn't find them. Once again nature prevailed. When it got dark, they moved for the closest stream and worked their way backwards to the bunker, before bypassing and heading for the bushes. Lucky for them they had stayed only a day at camp and their strength led them to safety.

Whizz, an arrow shot past my head. I was so lost in my own thoughts that I had forgotten about the hunt. It was a clean shot of a rabbit. "Nice work, umm."

"Jack," proud as punch over his first kill in a while. "Now all we need is four more of these, and I can make a stew."

My tummy started to immediately rumble, and it was then that I was reminded that I hadn't had a good feed in a while.

We managed to collect three rabbits and a kangaroo on this hunt, which was not too bad considering the slim pickings in the forest. The walk back was silent, everyone lost in their own thoughts, so it wasn't long before we hit the rose bushes and had dinner cooking, ready for our first meal together.

I told them the story of how I escaped, and it wasn't long before Charlie was telling jokes and making the whole group laugh again. Something I hadn't heard in a while. I slept peacefully that night in the knowledge that I was safe and that the others were too.

Morning broke and it wasn't long before the camp was abuzz. It was time to delegate. Even though our group was smaller it was easy enough; Jack and Tom, hunters; Kendall and Simone, watchers, and Charlie and I mapping and scouting. It was an easy enough job, but it would be days before we found anything useful for our camp.

It was then we found the abandoned town. Completely abandoned. No sign of life for what seemed like months. The place had obviously been looted in the early days as anything of use was gone, but I did manage to find a few cans of tuna deep in someone's pantry. A lucky find. It wasn't long before we had settled into one of the rooms in a house the size of a mountain and picked our way through the tuna. "Why do you reckon this town hasn't been colonised yet?" I asked Charlie.

"Dunno. Maybe it's too far off the radar – too far to travel. I mean all of the roads in and out are covered with scrub now so the Theodoris obviously didn't care enough about it and the Razors, well you know what they're like… nomadic."

"I suppose so, bet it would have been a really nice place to live before the, you know, invasion."

"Yeah, out in the bush, quiet, not too many people."

"I think we should mark this on the map as a rest spot, for the clan, so that if they ever need respite this is a safe place to stop."

"OK, but let's check out the other houses first."

We scurried around looking for anything of use. I found a newer pair of cargo pants and a short coat, army green, so I put them on trading them for my tattered clothes. It wasn't long before we had stocked up and started heading back to base camp. The afternoon sun played amongst the trees allowing us to indulge in a beautiful day. The walk was tantalising, and we talked quietly about our childhoods. Charlie's was very different from mine but at least I got to know him somewhat better. He'd grown up in a colony way north of here. They were outfitted pretty well with lots of defence mechanisms in place. It wasn't until he reached the age of 20, he got raided, and by then he was too old to become part of the ranks, so he was enslaved by his group led by a gruff Razor, Sienna. He was one of the luckier ones. He was traded through different Razor camps until he came to be part of Kemp's camp.

"And here we are." I pointed to the map. "We found a new place which would be OK for a hideout on our travels." I showed the group on the map where the town lay. It wasn't marked on there as a town, but we knew where it was and that's all that mattered.

Jack and Tom had scored hugely and had buried the animals to keep them fresh nearby and there was nothing to report from Kendall and Simone. So, after long chats into the evening, we all went off to bed.

I was awoken by trampling nearby. It was dark so I could hear more clearly in the night's silence. Whispers came from the dark. Kendall stirred and I put my hand over her mouth beside me. It was definitely human because of the whispers but they weren't being all that quiet. I pulled a gun from beside Charlie and proceeded to the entrance of the rose bushes. Sliding under I could see more clearly now as the moon lit up the dark sky. There were three of them and they looked completely lost. No weapons that I could see. But I wasn't going to risk it. I stilled in my position and kept my gun pointed towards them. One of the men stopped and seemingly looked right at me but then continued in conversation beckoning the others to move forward towards the stream. I slid out from under my comfort and followed them silently, ever ready to shoot if necessary. They stopped and drank from the water. "We'll stay here tonight." The man said approvingly. And they lay down to sleep. I watched them for hours. Until the sun came up and they stirred. Two men and a woman. They fluffed about the stream washing their faces. One of the men was tall and muscular and the other was shorter, both had beards. The girl was a sight to see. She had beautiful long brown hair, a lean but curvy figure and eyes that pierced blue like the water beside her. Compelled, I couldn't help but step out of the bush into the light.

"Fuck, fuck, please, don't shoot. We're just passing through. We don't mean any harm." The shorter of the two started.

"Where are you from?" I found myself asking the questions as if I wasn't stupid enough already to reveal myself.

"We're from the southern sea."

"Heading?" More of a command.

"We don't really know. Anywhere that keeps us out of trouble. Please, we'll move on. We didn't realise anyone was here."

I felt a peace come over me and I knew that I had to ask them more questions.

Moving my gun between them I started, "Are you looking for a settlement?"

"No. No way. Our last settlement was burnt to the ground. We've been on the run ever since. This is the densest bush we could find, so we've been tracking this forest for days to stay out of the way of the Razors and the Theodoris."

We continued on with the conversation and I learnt that the tall man's name was Rudy, the shorter man Steve and the woman Hasani. I felt rude staring, but she was beautiful, I just had to know more about them, about her.

I beckoned for them, "Come, follow me."

I knew that I had promised the others not to let anyone in, but I had a feeling about these three. It somehow felt right.

Kendall was in the shadows behind me and it was then that she revealed herself. "Are you crazy? We just gone and done talking about this? No more people."

"Take a look at them, no kids, I've been watching them all night. They have no clue about hiding and are definitely not scouts."

"It doesn't matter, we can't give away our spot."

"I was just taking them to the clearing."

"Then what? Offer them a cup of tea? The others aren't going to like this."

Still whispering we continued our conversation. Hasani came up to me and touched my side. I nearly shot her on the spot. "Shit, don't sneak up on a person like that."

"Sorry, it's just that, can we leave now?"

"Please stay, we have food and water, you can join us for breakfast in the clearing if you like."

Kendall eyeballed me ferociously.

"Come."

They were trusting us just as much as we were them, I could see it in their eyes. They weren't sure which way to go.

Finally, Hasani resolved to follow and the men came too.

I organised for the food to be brought to the clearing and man were the others pissed about it.

"What about your last gut feeling?" Charlie reminded me.

"This is different. I know that we were meant to cross paths."

We monitored them for days before the others started to trust them. Simone was asking a million questions and I just sat back quietly watching Hasani's movements. The way she held her hands, the way she spoke in a slightly different accent to us. I felt a shyness settle over me when she caught me out. It was then that I would only catch glimpses of her dark hair flowing in the breeze or those blue eyes sparkling around the grounds. She was a sight to behold and I was ruined by her.

It would be weeks before they would be allowed to form part of our camp and by then we had known everything there is to know about their last settlement, about life in the south, about fishing and swimming in the ocean. They had been given jobs as hunters for their fishing and navigation skills. I had to train them in the art of the bow. It was funny at first, although with a straight face, I held the laughter within. Was I this bad when I started? They really had no clue how to use a bow but neither did I and I reminded myself of this, composed myself and continued with the lesson. Of course, I needed to be close to Hasani so I would at every moment take a chance and show her how to hold and release the bow. I would come up close behind her and hold her arms into position. Firmly grasping them to help make the bow and string not so flimsy. Then I would pull back her hand on the string and come close into her cheek, breathe out across her ear and tell her to release. She was getting better and as the days went on, we became close. I would go on fishing trips with them and she would show me how to bait the line properly, which made a huge difference to the art of catching many more fish.

Chapter 17

But it was shortly after fishing that we connected. It was in the depths of the cool blue waters that we would talk of days gone past, of her family and where she had grown up, where she had moved to and how they had managed to escape the clutches of the Razors many times. They had been free all of this time. Continuing to move to wherever the breeze took them, and it had worked. All the while I would watch her petite mouth move slowly, while she brushed back her hair and I would take in the curiosity of it all. She was lean but toned and as the water rushed over her body shivers would be sent down my spine while butterflies danced joyously in my stomach. It was an unfamiliar feeling for me, and I tried to push it aside, but I would find my thoughts drifting back to her, images of the past flashing through my mind and I felt content. It was a worthwhile distraction from the monotony of what had become our days at camp. But my question was, did she feel the same?

It wasn't until night watch some months later that my question would be answered. Hasani and I were on together and as we looked into the clear night; I felt a sudden urgency sweep over me. She looked so beautiful under the stars' gaze and I was almost sure now that she had some sort of feelings for me. So, I took a leap of faith and slowly edged towards her. Startled she edged back but I could see a longing in her eyes. I had committed too much already so I leant forward and as my lips met hers, I kissed her gently. She did not kiss back but rather embraced my lips knowingly. I couldn't help but sneak another but this time her lips moved in unison with mine. We improvised back and forth until I was laying on top of her on the damp ground and we were in a full-scale embrace. I moved my hand over her body, feeling every ounce of it. Taking it all in as I went. It was magical and we were finally together as one.

Life is incredibly feeble and with this monotony, I needed something to allow me to feel again. Something worth living for, something to allow me freedom of expression from this isolation. I had no idea that I was in fact feeling lonely. Craving intimacy. But there's always something about life and its existence. It knows when to give you what you need. It allows for love, even amongst all of this anguish and sorrow. Out of the shadows comes something greater, something bigger than myself and I would embrace it with everything that I have.

Just then Kendall interrupted my thoughts. "Oda, are you coming on the hunt with us today? Or are you doing more scouting?"

"Scouting." I knew that this would give me more time with Hasani.

"OK, so we're heading out now, we'll see you at nightfall."

"Stay safe."

"You too."

Picking up the compass, I went to find Hasani but she was nowhere to be found. I couldn't yell because that would be too conspicuous, so I walked the boundary until I found her in the lake. She was swimming, looking like there was not a care in the world. Her brunette hair was drifting behind her as she went, fanning the water surrounding her. I stopped and watched for a moment. Mesmerised by the simplicity of it all.

She was so beautiful. So carefree. So life-inducing.

I called to her and she beckoned me to come swimming with her. Was it too risky? She beckoned again. I couldn't resist and slowly stripped down until I was naked before her. I dove into the water and concluded that this was the best place for me at this time. Amongst the cool water, allowing the light breeze to flow over me as I swam towards her. We gazed at each other for what seemed like an eternity. Lust overflowing in my body and love in my heart. How can this be that I have fallen so utterly? I assess the situation. Thinking about the repercussions for our group. For our safety. It is then I looked around. Was there someone in the bushes? I am paranoid about plans gone past. But then she breaks me from it, with one single touch on my shoulder I am risen from my cognition and brought back into her world. "Where are you?" I shrug as if nothing had happened and wait eagerly for her next move. She flinched and slowly moved her body towards mine. I was caught in an embrace and we hugged for moments in time. Life went on and we were stuck in a silent picture as I was encapsulated by her eyes. I moved closer to her and as I did, she grabbed me around the waist and pulled me closer. I was trapped in her intentions. I wanted it more than she could ever imagine. All of it. The warm embrace, the loving glances, the forever. I wrapped these into my mouth and upon her lips I place these thoughts. She returned it with passion and it was there in that creek that we fought for each other. In a full-scale embrace, I moved to pull her closer to the small of her back. She received me and I her.

We moved towards the bank and laid upon the cool grass still in a close embrace. I rested her down and began to caress her body, inch by inch I left no space un-kissed. Starting at her ear, I breathed wildly past it, as the passion lifted, I could feel her heart beating ever so heavily. I moved to kiss the outer skin where the beating lies and with it, my heart raced through time. Moving gently now I whispered in her ear, "You are beautiful." Then caressed it gently as I moved my hand over her body. Her form was covered in tiny bumps and I responded by touching her breast ever so gently with the tips of my lips, sending air over them as they cooled and dried. She responded immediately and her nipple elongated. I moved to the other, this time biting gently, I teased her. My hands moved down her thighs as I motioned. I grazed over her vagina and could feel the wetness prevalent between her thighs and I was ever present of the wetness between mine. I began to kiss her abdomen, gently trying to catch every bump I could until I reached her hip bone. It is then I moved wildly to her lips and kissed with intent as I pushed my thumbs into her hip and caressed the outsides with my fingertips. I was once again completely engrossed in her eyes. My hands couldn't help but work their way towards her vagina and there I played with the wetness forming outside. She groaned for more, but I continued to tease. I was mapping her body. Then in one movement I spun her on top of me and rolled to be in between her thighs. She gasped ever so softly, and it is there I began to play gently with her clitoris; using my tongue to softly swirl around the outsides allowing her to feel every essence of it. My fingers still softly playing with the outside of her vagina, my other hand caressing her hip through to her buttocks. Slipping in and out I allow myself to slowly feel her inside. Not enough to engage pleasure but enough to stir the waters. She began to moan so I began to lick her clitoris more passionately following the patterns of her moaning. Speeding up, I pulled down on her and was now fully inside of her. She moved her hips spiritedly as I enthused in and out of her, every now and then pausing at her g spot. It was then that I rolled her again onto the ground and continued to caress her breasts with my other hand. She was allowing herself to be free and began to shake. Her hips pushing against me and me moving more freely inside of her. And just as she was about to come, I pulled out, still licking, and again pushed in hard against her. She screamed in pleasure as she came all over my hand. And I was happy. I laid on top of her limp body. She was in a far-away land, so I listened to her heart beat gently in her chest.

It must've been midday and we still hadn't scouted but to feel carefree was a much-needed thing for me right then. The sun was shining through the trees playfully casting shadows from the canopy above us and butterflies twisted and turned in the cool breeze. I let out a deep breath and breathed in the surrounding air. Somehow, Hasani refocused and was back with me, we laid there with her head on my shoulder and me laying on my back. We stayed there for what seemed like an eternity before the sun dipped behind the mountain to the west. It was then that we get dressed and headed back to camp.

"Hey, how did you go?" It was Kendall.

"Yeah good," I lied. "And you?"

"We managed to find enough for the next week, so we can chill out on the hunting for a while."

Damn, I thought. *That means that they will be spending more time around the camp.*

"That's good news," I lied again.

It was like every moment was precious and I wanted to spend it all with her. We would have to arrange it so that we were both on scouting the next day. But for the moment, I would have to live with the cheeky glances from across the room and the ever-so-fine touches as we brushed past each other. The night was young, but I couldn't wait until morning, so I went to bed straight after dinner.

The morning could not come soon enough. I could feel the sunrise well before it had arrived, and it was then I arose early to swim in the lake. It was still dark, and yesterday's plight was still on my lips. So, I drifted through the reeds relishing the memories. When dawn appeared, I got dressed and moved back to camp where Jack and Tom were already setting up breakfast and discussing the day's plans. The camp was alive and so was I. I spiritedly spoke, "Good morning."

"And what's so special about today?" A cheeky response came from Jack.

"Nothing, just happy to be alive."

"Good, well, grab some berries and plums for the table."

I moved quickly and managed to suppress a smile as I passed Hasani. "Good morning."

"Good morning," returned from her supple lips and a smile soon followed.

I couldn't help but flick one back.

"Plums and berries," I started, not sure if it was embarrassment or happiness that had started me.

After breakfast, we gathered around to listen for the list of jobs. Kendall and Jack were on watch, Simone and Tom were on cleaning the camp, Charlie, Rudy and Steve were on watch in the trees and Hasani and I were on scouting. I tried to contain myself but the excitement I felt could not hide the lingering smile. Hasani smiled back and I reached for the compass.

We walked for a while in silence. It wasn't awkward but rather presented a knowing. I was following in her footsteps, so I had a pretty good view. We got to a familiar bend in the river and I knew that there was an offshoot up ahead with a small waterfall. So, I grabbed her gently motioning to move left. It would be at least half an hour before I could take her in my arms and kiss her eagerly. Our lives entwining in a single moment. Everything disappeared from sight and there was just us and the coolness of the waterfall beside us. Playfully, I pushed her under, and she gasped at the temperature of it. Her hair fell lower down her back as the water pulled us. I walked under the waterfall to join her and breathe in the coolness of it. Pushing her up against the wall we let the water fall over us as we kissed passionately. It was there that I could feel it. An unfamiliar feeling, a lightness in my soul. Like the burden just lifted and I didn't even know it was there. I leaned in closer and started to kiss her neck, letting the water fall over us. She groaned back with eagerness. It was then she grabbed me and pushed me up against the rock wall. I was so full of surprise that I let her kiss me taking in my earlobes and neck. A sudden rush came over me and I was aware that I was blushing, but I didn't want it to stop. It was the first time I had allowed anyone to be with me since Kemp and I was a little dubious, but I was so encapsulated by her that I felt safe in her arms. She moved to my breasts caressing them with her hands, motioning in circles through my loose-fitting top. They immediately responded. I pulled her in closer kissing her hard on the lips. Walking her backwards, I moved to the mossy undertow close to the waterfall and laid her gently on the grass. We played rolling on the grass, kissing, touching gently at first but then more intently.

Hasani laid on top of me where she began to kiss me in between the hips moving my top slowly upwards as she traced my body. I was naked before her, so I sat her up in my lap and kissed her collarbones. I slowly lifted her top from her charting her upper body with my tongue and lips soft on her forgiving skin. She arched her back as I kissed her nipples, moving them between my tongue and lips. She started to move her hips against my pelvis which made me begin to get wet. Rolling her onto her back, I slowly removed her pants, kissing her hips through to her thighs whilst pushing my hand hard against her calf and onto her feet. She flipped me again and turned on top of me. I could see the wetness between her thighs and lifted my head slightly to meet her. She bent slightly to meet me. Soon enough, we were both entwined in each other. I could feel her licking my clitoris and it made me wild. Life grew inside of me and I returned the favour softly suckling on her clit. Moving between that and gently caressing her breasts. We were moving in unison, my pelvis tilted slightly, and her hips rotated, gently moving with my licking. It was becoming too intense and I felt her slip her fingers inside of me and with that, I let out a moan and lost concentration for a moment. Her fingers were like an electric spark igniting a desire inside of me. I wanted more. Regaining focus, I continued to kiss and lick her and then returning the favour, I took two of my fingers and gently slipped them inside of her. She groaned and we were both moaning together and just before she came, I pulled out and moved her on top of my hips. It was there I continued to play around the outside of her clitoris and soon, spiritedly, turning circles on her right breast. She was moaning again so I slowly inserted two fingers inside of her pushing towards her G-spot. It was at that moment that I was once again encapsulated by her eyes. Looking deeply into them, I began to lightly thrust deep inside of her. She responded by moving her hips back and forth on top of me. She leaned back and inserted her fingers inside of me and we were moving in unison. I was beginning to shake, and she responded with deep moans. It wasn't long before I could feel my head get hot and I came under the pressure. She continued to wildly thrust her body on me until she began to shake and come on top of me. We laid there for a while in each other's arms. I could feel my heart beating in my chest and in the aftermath, I basked in the beauty of the sun. It wasn't long before we moved to the waterfall and washed each other under the cascading spring.

Chapter 18

We were scouting until the sun was high in the sky before I found the tracks. They were much larger than those of animals but were so subtle in their nature. A little to the left or right and I would have missed them entirely. I motioned for Hasani to be quiet before engaging in the trail. The greenery to the left was trampled into the debris below and the density of the forest had been lessened by broken twigs and leaves afloat. What, or more to the point who was it that had trekked through here not so long ago? We cautiously urged forward knives at the ready and I listened for any suspicious sounds. Nothing. They must have passed through days earlier. Moments down the track I heard a rustle from above then a smack to the back of the head that left me reeling. I turned to face a man, not that old, hairy-faced and lean in figure. I swung the knife at him and Hasani stood at the ready, he dodged and gave me another whack on the left arm. This guy could fight. Not that I was a fighter, after all, the only training I'd had was at the Razor's camp. I sized him up. Razor? Whatever the case, we had a brawl on our hands. He pulled a knife out of his belt and we circled each other like sharks to its prey. Testing his reflexes, I lunged forward, he quickened back with a swing of the knife just missing my abdomen. He was quick. I swapped my footing to be on par with his and again attempted to cut him. It was a success I managed to draw blood from his arm. But not without the repercussion of him drawing blood from my upper thigh. "What are you doing out here?" I found myself questioning in the midst of our duel. If he was a Razor by now, there would have been a whole scouting troop upon us.

"None of your business," he scowled back. Looks like the duelling would continue. He lunged at me drawing blood from my arm. "You're obviously not a Razor so what are you doing this far out?"

He scowled again. "I'm not one of those filthy mongrels, I stick to myself and that seems to get me through just fine."

I stopped to process. Alone. How could he still be alive?

It was then I noticed the scarring on his arms and legs.

"Well, I'm not a Razor either so why don't we call it quits and just chat for a minute?"

"Chat, I'm going to kill you. I don't know what's behind your corner and one last Razor on this Earth, in my opinion, is for the best."

I slowly lowered my knife to the ground and beckoned Hasani to do the same. "We didn't come here for a fight. We just saw the tracks and…"

"They're there to lead you to me."

"You mean you trap people and then kill them?"

"Razors, I trap Razors."

"Well, like I said before, we are not Razors and see now, I'm unarmed. Put the knife away."

"No way am I doing that, how do I know there's not a dozen filthy mongrels just yonder?"

"I guess you don't, but would a Razor back down from a fight? Think about it."

He stopped momentarily and seemingly rationalised the situation, but he still didn't back down. That's all we need a rogue in our neck of the woods. Then he did something I never thought he would. He must have spotted it.

"Shit, you're the girl."

"What?"

"The girl with the golden neck."

My shirt must have slipped in the kafuffle. I covered it up.

"I've heard about you. The Razors have been looking all over for you. Even have a reward for whoever finds you."

Fuck, now I've got a bounty hunter on the loose.

"How have you managed to escape all of this time?"

I took it as a rhetorical question.

He lowered his knife. "Well, any enemy of the Razors is a friend of mine."

I definitely wasn't expecting that.

"What's your name?" I found myself asking.

"Sam, and you?"

"Oda, this is Hasani."

We talked for hours about his life, the fights he'd had and the colonies he had destroyed, small ones of course and it got me thinking about how we needed to be the catalyst for change. If one man could do it, then maybe the rest of us could be trained and also start fighting back. I mean we couldn't hide all of our lives, contained in one part of the forest. I felt empowered by this one man, it was like a spark was reignited in me. Like I had a purpose in life again. I invited him back to the field where we took all of our newbies and got Hasani to get the others while I stayed and listened to his stories, where he got his scars from and where he'd learnt how to track. It was just him and his dad and it was his father who had taught him the skills needed for survival in this new world. His dad was also a ranger much like himself, together they had killed many Razors but unfortunately, he was taken, and as Sam watched on from the bushes, his dad was killed at the camp. So that left Sam, alone.

I heard a familiar rustle in the bushes it was the others and I could tell that Sam was getting nervous. He reached for his knife, but I motioned that it was OK. Still wary he rested his hand on it. Jack was first to arrive, and he looked at me startled. "Who's this?"

"It's OK, his name is Sam."

Jack lowered the gun that was pointed at Sam and they glared at each other for seemingly moments in time. The others followed through wary of the new comer. We stood in silence for a while before Simone asked Sam where he was from. They knew they had the upper hand with the small stock of arsenal that we had so questions kept firing until the mood lightened and Sam was talking freely amongst the group.

"Sam fights off the Razors," I piped up.

Tom interjected, "How can you do that? They are so strong?"

"It's all about the timing." Sam started. "You need to map out their camp first and in order to do that you need to draw out their scouts. Pick them off one by one then you have easy access to the camp. First of all, I never use a gun. Too much noise. I sneak in at night and tent by tent I slit their throats. The trick is to pick the weaker Razor camps. The bigger ones, I avoid."

"Maybe we could help?" I started.

"What, and get caught again?" Steve remarked.

"We won't get caught if we do it Sam's way, and that means we will have fewer colonies to worry about."

"I don't know. I like life now."

"Yeah, but what happens when the Razors scour this area and we can't hunt or worse we get caught again? Wouldn't you rather try and fight back, than lay victim to the inevitability of them finding us? I mean, they already found us at our last base. It could quite easily happen here."

This wouldn't be an easy task to convince the others. They had already been through enough trauma.

"I am sick of being the victim in all of this. I need to fight back and if that means the possibility of death then at least I died trying to make the world a better place."

"Alright, settle down, Oda," Steve responded.

It was silent for a while until Kendall spoke, "I'm in. I mean I can't stand the anxiety of waiting to be discovered again. It's always right there with me in the back of my mind. You're right, we need to do something."

Murmurs could be heard amongst the rest of the crew. They weren't all impressed with the situation. I knew that I needed to give them time. Meanwhile, Kendall and I could begin training in one-on-one combat. There was no time to waste so I asked Sam if he would train us and he agreed. We learned the art of hand-to-hand combat whenever there was a spare moment from our duties. Sam was still not allowed into the rose bushes, so he was on night watch a lot and slept out in the fields during the day. The afternoons were when most of the camp had returned and it was a quiet time, so we trained and trained hard. The exercise was making us fitter, stronger, and quicker.

Chapter 19

Hasani and I grew closer, more intimate. Every chance we had together we were. Whilst out scouting we happened upon a beautiful field of daisies and Hasani went running in the field. I watched her, mesmerised by the graceful movement of her body. She started to dance swaying with the gentle breeze, arms and eyes pointed to the sky. I sat down in the field fixated on her. She danced towards me and we lay down in the field together lightly kissing each other on the lips, bodies entangled with each other. Our own dance. Lust grew in my eyes as I lifted her shirt gently caressing her breasts with my fingertips. Her nipples hardened with the play. The intensity of her kisses grew with every stroke. Wild and passionate. I moved lower, familiarising myself with her abdomen, playfully lingering at her hips, pushing gently into the parts that tickled her. She too was now in performance with my breasts, teasing them softly. I could feel the ever-present butterflies growing in my stomach and a familiar feeling of pulsing pleasure in my vagina. I wanted her so badly. I lingered on her pelvic bone before slowly lowering her jeans. Kissing her thighs in between I moved in circular motions towards her clitoris. I lifted her hood and continued to circle tracing the outskirts of it; until it started to swell with delight.

I loved being here, right where she liked it most. Her moans rang out into the abyss and I had a sense of happiness within. Love had engulfed me, and its tight grip held me close. I began to lick faster, and her moaning increased. She was enjoying every moment of me and so was I. Holding off, I slowed and quickened all to keep her at her peak. It wasn't until I started sucking on her clitoris, did she start to transcend and with one last breath, she orgasmed. We lay in the field until the sun was high in the sky then continued scouting.

We entered unfamiliar territory, so we needed to be extra careful. I pulled my knife and Hasani did the same. We quietly and effortlessly moved throughout the bush careful not to make any sound. There were rabbits and deer, but we ignored them and continued to climb north-east until we came to a cliff face. We were set high in the mountains and below was an expanse of forest, as far as the eye could see. I sat dangling my legs over the edge looking for any sign of life in the distance. Then I saw it. Smoke. A fire had been lit below. "Who do you think it could be?" Hasani questioned.

"Could be anyone," I responded. "All I know is that this is an excellent spot for a lookout."

I marked it on the map and after a while, we returned to camp with the news.

"They are still pretty far off our camp, but it's worth a look." I proposed to the group.

We hadn't had much training, but we knew the basics of how to trap a person. The only problem was could I kill one, again? I mustered up all of the anger inside I could and reasoned that it was for the cause, so logically it was the right thing to do. Less of them, more chance of survival for us. It seemed that not everyone felt the same way, but they did think it was worth a look. To see who was actually out there.

Sam, Kendall, Hasani, Charlie and I set out the next day this time mirroring the mountains' lower edges so as not to end up on the cliff. The smoke was drawing nearer so we decided to spread out and Sam went on ahead to see if there were any scouts. It was moments before we heard a kafuffle in the bushes ahead, then an "All clear," from Sam. I walked towards him not knowing what to expect. "Scout 0, me 1," Sam cheekily said, amused at himself. Before long, he had them all down and we were sitting on the outskirts of a camp. There were four tents in total and about 20 Razors busy around the campsite. What looked like the chief was sitting in the middle feasting on what looked like the leg of a deer. We watched them until nightfall and when they had retreated to their tents Sam sprang into action. He had been counting them off as they went. "Four in this tent, five in…" he continued explaining where each of them had migrated to. Sam told us to stay put and within moments he was heading to the first tent. We watched as he scurried between each tent, then retreated back to us. "And that is how you clear a Razor camp."

I couldn't believe my eyes, he was like night's death. Alone. He cleared an entire camp. I was shocked. "Is it safe to go in?"

"Sure is," he responded proudly.

I walked into the first tent finding three dead men. In the second, I found more. In the third, there was death but there was also life. Two girls were tied up. They were silent. Unsure. I asked them what their names were, and they responded Sally and Mae. "Do you want to come with me?

You will be safe." They nodded tentatively and I released them from their bondages. All in all, we rescued five people; another girl by the name of Sandy and two men Robert and Cameron were also at camp. We burnt the site to the ground, grabbed as many supplies as we could carry and then took the rescued back to the field near our home and they slept out under the stars for their first night of freedom. It was still too risky to give away our hiding spot. Plus, Sam watched over them, so they were safe enough.

Morning broke the dark sky, Jack cooked up a feed fit for a king and everyone enjoyed breakfast in the field. Mae a skinny, frail blonde-haired girl spoke first. "Who are you?"

"We are just like you, survivors," I responded.

"But how did you get away?" This time Sally spoke.

"We all have our stories; over time you may learn them. But for now, you all need to rest."

We left the newcomers with Sam in the field and went about our daily routines. This time I was on watch with Kendall. We stationed ourselves in the gum tree overlooking the valley and spoke freely.

"So, I've noticed a few things," Kendall started.

I couldn't help but hold back a smirk, but it must have been all over my face.

"So, it's true?"

"Whatever do you mean?" I responded calmly.

"You and Hasani?" She probed further. "Are you an item?"

"I wouldn't say that."

"Bullshit, it's written all over your face."

"Why, what have you seen?"

"The long gazes, the days out with her with no report of finding anything. C'mon Oda, you can tell me."

"I think I'm in love, Kendall." She looked at me in shock. "No seriously, I think I'm actually in love."

"Oh, Oda, I am so jealous. I wish that I had that kind of thing in my life. It would make it so much more worthwhile."

"Yeah, I don't know how it happened. I've liked her from the first moment I laid eyes on her. She is beautiful, intelligent, creative, and endearing, all of the things I want in a partner. I am so lucky to have found her."

"Lucky, damn right you are and how does she feel about you?"

"I don't know. I mean we've, you know." I gave her a glance and she giggled back at me.

"Well, she obviously likes you."

"How so?"

"Every chance possible she's where you are."

"You think?"

"Yeah, it's obvious. I'm not the only one who's noticed. Simone said something to me the other day."

"Shit. Does the whole campsite know?"

"I don't think so. I think the boys haven't noticed."

"Well, let's keep it that way at least until it's all official OK?"

Kendall nodded and we drifted off into our own thoughts for a while. All I could think of was Hasani's long brown hair, her beautiful smile and those bright blue eyes. You couldn't wipe the smile off my face even if you tried.

Soon enough, Simone and Tom came to relieve us of our duty, and we ambled on back to the field where Sam and the newcomers were.

I got talking to Sandy, a tall, lean girl with a cynical smile, lazily I asked how she got to be held at the Razor camp. It was a familiar story of a raid on her camp and she had been taken hostage to be a cook and cleaner at the camp with Robert and Cameron. It seems she had been there for years with no hope of ever escaping. She was so glad to be rid of the camp and was highly thankful that we had come when we did. I guess that's the whole purpose of this. Not just to rid the world of Razors but to rescue the innocent who are caught in their webs as well. To build a strong community of people who wanted to rebuild and hopefully get back at the Razors and make a difference. The only problem was that we weren't warriors. We weren't brought up to kill people like Sam. Animals, yes but people? I mean, I've done it before, but I didn't cope. Overcoming this would be the hardest part of my life. We continued training well into the afternoon.

With the camp filling up so quickly we needed to find better hiding spots and possibly even split up to cover more ground so Hasani and I set out early in the morning to find locations for the newcomers. They couldn't stay out in the open like they were or else sooner or later a Razor scout or Theodoris soldiers would find them. We headed west past the bunker and into the wilder bush. There were loads of lantana to work our way through but no clean hiding spots. Smaller alcoves nested in the vast mountains and small waterfalls trickled from above. We rounded the corner and there it was. A cave – not unlike our own – covered by lantana – the perfect spot. Hard to get to but easy to escape from.

Inside the glow worms lit up the cave like the night sky, vines circulating the cave and in its dampness I felt inspired. I pushed Hasani's face hard against the cave wall, holding her arms behind her back. Pinning her in place with my knee to her thigh. In contrast, I breathed gently past her right ear. She tried to move but I had her held tight. I slowly lifted her arms above her head and bound her to the vines dangling overhead. My hands found their way to her shoulders and as I pushed her closer to the wall, I could hear a storm brewing outside and its power consumed me, echoing in our bodies as we pushed and pulled at each other, me overpowering and Hasani resisting. But to no avail.

I bit her neck drawing blood and she winced with the pleasure of it all. A crack of thunder woke me from my obsession commanding me to kiss further down her neck to the opening of her shoulders from her shirt. A flicker of light raised the standard sending a temporary blinding light through my eyes mirroring the electricity brewing in the nerves in my body. I am motivated to push harder, and I kissed in unforgiving waves against her back. Another crash encompasses my body commanding; almost as if Mother Nature is urging, encouraging, even demanding me. I pulled her close to me and caressed her breasts harshly pulling at her nipples but softly kissing her ear lobes, whispering her yearnings in her ear. I pushed my hands down her abdomen towards her jeans and with one swift motion, I unbuttoned and pulled them from her – exposing her to the elements. It was there, I wrenched on the inside of her thighs kissing her back and biting intermitted as I go. Another crash and I was moved to play with her clitoris stirring in circles with my fingers and she began to moan. Above me, I found another vine and pulled it low. I wrapped it around her neck, loosely at first. Then I turned her to see into her eyes, playfully, I tightened and loosened the vine around her neck allowing her to feel the pressure of it all, all the while searching her eyes. She was searching mine back and the flickering of the lightening showed me the spirit in them. This time, I was in the mood to fuck. So, I pushed my fingers forcefully inside of her and tightened the vine as I went, she gasped with desire. Moving in and out I got faster and harder and with every push, I would pull the vine harder around her neck, then loosen it letting my fingers slow. My body was full of excitement as I watched her writhe in pleasure. She moaned harder as I pushed deeper and soon, she was beginning to shake. It was then I pulled the vine tight around her throat and held it there until she came. With the vine pulled tight, her eyes were bewitching, forever staring, they then slowly faded as she succumbed to the pressure. I caught her as she fell, and the storm eased as her body went limp. Holding her close, I untied the vines binding her hands and lay her gently in my arms on the ground. She awoke shortly after, smiling at me with perfection. Tired from the endeavour, she lay there for a while and I couldn't help but gaze at her while I played with her hair. Perfect spot for a hideout.

We ventured back to the group with our newfound place in tow. The sun had broken through the clouds, so steam was slowly rising from the ground surrounding us. It was a mean feat to get back through all of the lantana but there was excitement in the air, and I couldn't wait to tell the others about this new, now magical, sanctuary. As the sun set, we entered camp the others were already eating so we joined them and told them about the new place.

"Just west of here," I explained. "Loads of lantana… good for coverage… glow worms in the cave." And it continued until I had painted a picture of this soon to be dwelling. It was then a matter of divvying up everyone.

"Well, how do we do this?" Charlie questioned.

Tom responded, "Why not the new ones in one camp and the old in another?"

"But how are we going to train? Too hard. We need to have an even mixture."

"How about half and half?" Kendall piped in.

"Well, it's not that far that we couldn't have contact with each other. Would it be best to think about this from the perspective of who wants to raid the Razors and who wants to remain as a support back here?" Sam had some reasoning in his question. That way training can continue for those who wanted to raid, and the others could hunt, gather and look after the camps.

"I agree with Sam. We need to keep the ones being trained together plus have some support in the same site, and those who don't want to raid then they can stay at the other campsite. What do you think?"

"Makes sense to me," Kendall interjected.

There was a general consensus and a nod from most people. So now it was a matter of dividing the two groups. Kendall was the first to raise her hand for the raid, then Charlie, Tom, Cameron and Hasani. Of course, Sam and I were already in. So that left Simone, Jack, Rudy, Steve, Sam, Mae, Sandy and Robert. Robert being a cook stayed with us and Simone was to keep watch, all of the others were to go to the other camp.

Early the next morning we rolled into action and I took the others to the new camp site to set up. We stopped by the bunker and took more supplies from there to the cave. Jack had set up camp before, so he was in charge of preparations and very quickly started ordering people to and fro.

As we walked back, I looked up into the beautiful clear sky admiring the sun as it pirouetted through the trees and onto my face. I squinted through its glare and admired its courage to rise and fall every day. Soon enough we were back at camp training in the clearing. We were getting pretty good at hand-to-hand combat too. On top of what I had learnt at the Razor camp, I could now disarm someone with a knife to my throat and was learning the art of sneaking up on someone. Sam was way too good, he got me every time but me, I hadn't got him once yet.

Soon enough though it became part of our daily ritual, wherever we were we were in training. At breakfast, Kendall managed to sneak up on me and put me on the ground. It was now time to be hypervigilant all of the time as the seriousness became relevant because it was only a matter of time before we would have to put these skills into practise. And the time came soon enough.

Chapter 20

It was a routine day and Kendall and I were out scouting. We had headed further west past the other camp. I was mapping out the next mountain when it happened. Kendall was on watch, but it didn't matter they came from the trees above, and dropped right down on top of us knocking the compass from my hand. I rolled on the ground and sprung to life. He was tall and muscular but that didn't scare me. I was used to Sam. Knives at the ready we circled each other; I could see Kendall circling the other. Lunging forward I swung, only to nip his shoulder as he stepped back from me. *Razor*, I thought. He eyed me, smiling widely. "C'mon girl, let's see if you've got more than that." He came in closer and I swung again, this time he grabbed my arm and swung me around so that my back was to him, but just before he drew the knife to my throat I kicked backwards right into his nether regions. He doubled over in pain and I turned to knee him in the head. Now he was on the ground but not defeated. His knife-wielding wildly as I tried to get closer to him. He rose, now fuming and he lunged at me intently. Catching my arm as he went. I was now bleeding from the force of it, but the adrenaline kept me focussed. As he lunged again, I ducked and grabbed him around the waist, pulling him in close I held my knife to his neck, and then it happened. It must have been the training, I cut him open and he fell to the ground. Surprised at first, I stood there staring at his lifeless body. But Kendall's screams brought me back to life. She was pinned to the ground the Razor on top of her. I snuck up behind him and with one swift motion cut him too.

There was blood everywhere, so much blood. I turned and vomited right where I stood, the adrenaline wearing off slightly. Kendall got to her feet and questioned, "Are you alright?"

"Sure," I replied wiping the vomit from my mouth. "We need to get out of here before others come. Quick, help me hide the bodies." We hid them amongst the thorns of a nearby lantana bush and hurried back to camp.

"We need to act now before they notice they're missing and alert the others," Sam motioned. "It's dusk so we can get there in the dark and find the other scouts. How big was the camp?"

"Fuck. We didn't get that close. Two of them were enough for us," I replied.

"Grab your gear, we're moving out."

And with that, we were on our way back to the killing field.

I was still shaking from earlier that day, so the walk was arduous. I just needed more energy, but I felt lethargic. C'mon Oda, get it together, I tried to pep myself up. Before I knew it, we were there.

"This is where we hid the bodies."

Sam was already on the lookout moving in the shadows from tree to tree. "There won't be any in this area or else you would have known about it, but we can never be too safe." He reasoned. "C'mon, let's go."

I took a look at the spew I'd left on the ground no more than a metre away and felt the all too familiar feeling in my stomach. I choked it down and kept on following. It wasn't long before Sam stopped in his tracks. He pointed up ahead and sure enough another Razor was sitting perched in the tree above. Tom took his bow this time and aimed directly at him. It was a chance; one wrong hit and all of the other Razors would be alerted. "Steady now," Sam insisted. He pulled the line into his cheek and let out a deep breath. The arrow released and speared the Razor through the throat. He fell silently from the tree but landed with a huge thud. "Fuck." An arrow flew past my head. Then another. A holler went out and I knew we were soon to be surrounded. "Get to cover!" I yelled. We all disappeared behind trees and bushes and before I knew it, they were upon us. Bow and arrows trained all over. It was Tom who sent the next arrow flying, right into the quadricep of a nearby Razor. An arrow flew back. A near miss. They then engaged in combat. My breathing sped up as one brushed straight past the tree I was standing at. How did I not see her? Luckily, she hadn't noticed me yet, so I crept up behind her. My foot crunched on a stick and I lunged at her as she turned towards me, I punched her square in the face knocking the bow from her hand. She took a few steps back but was not fazed by the attack. She punched back and I blocked her with my left. We were in a boxing scuffle. I moved forward to punch and she dodged hitting me right under the ribs. I doubled back and blocked the next serious of onslaughts. Left, right, left. I pulled her in, holding her, trying to squeeze the life out of her but she was too strong, using her hip she threw me to the ground. On all fours, I gained my balance, but she had closed in on me, my jaw felt like it had broken, she'd hit me hard across the face. Blood poured from my mouth and I felt a little dazed. Then it came, another from the left. I didn't have the time or sense to block. I was still startled by the first punch. More blood fell from my mouth. Then she was upon me. First, I felt the tightness around my throat, then the arm to the back of my head. I pulled at the arm around my throat, but she had me in tight, lifting me from the ground. Gasping for air I kicked at her, but it was to no avail, she was much stronger than me, but the fight hadn't left me yet. I continued to twist and turn my body using my elbows to drive into her ribs. Every now and then she loosened her grip but quickly regained it. I started to feel light-headed and the energy to fight back was draining from my body. Was this the end? It darkened around me.

"Oda. Oda, wake up. Oda." I could hear a familiar voice calling me. Then I felt my body shaking. My awareness was returning, and I was beginning to feel an ache in my head. "What happened?"

Charlie responded, "That bitch almost killed you. If it wasn't for Simone, you'd be dead right now. She had you in a headlock." The world around me became clearer but with every moment a new pain could be felt. I spat the blood from my mouth and turned to Charlie. "Is everyone OK?"

"Trust you to think of that in a moment like this. A few scratches and cuts but yeah, we wasted those Razors. Are you right to move? We have to get going. Sam's already on the scout. It seems that there is no camp nearby, so he's gone to find it before they figure out their scouts are missing."

"I'll come too. I can help."

"No, Oda, you can barely stand. Hasani said that she'll stay with you. We've found a hiding spot in the bushes nearby. We'll come and get you when it's over." And with that, he was gone.

Hasani dragged me to my feet and placed her arm under me and we slowly walked to the nearby bushes. Straight lines were hard at this point, but she got me there and placed me sitting in front of her. Time stood still as she played with my hair and kissed me gently on the head. Blackness engulfed me as I fell asleep.

I woke still in the same position. Hasani had held me for what seemed like a lifetime. "How's your head?"

"I have the worst headache you could imagine, and man am I sore."

"You sure got a beating. You are lucky to be alive. If it wasn't for Simone, I mean, you wouldn't be…" She started to cry.

"It's OK. I'm OK. Plus, I get to spend some extra time with you."

I kissed her on the lips. And couldn't help but steal another.

The sound of rustling approached, and it wasn't long before Sam poked his head into the bushes. "Success," he boasted. It seems they stumbled upon a small group of Razors camped out in the bushes. So, after taking out the scouts they were able to pick them off with ease. I was feeling much better, so we walked back to camp. Exhausted I slept until well after noon. It's funny this time round I didn't get any nightmares from killing those two guys. It's almost as if I had dissociated from it all. That I had justified it because they were the enemy, they were the killers, and they destroyed my family and the family of everyone in our encampment, so they deserved it.

I woke to the crew talking of stories from the night before. Of how they scouted the camp and were able to silently kill off some of the Razors, fought victoriously with others and used their bow and arrows to slay the rest. It was a success as Sam had said. I couldn't focus on much, I think that I had a concussion from the night before, but I caught parts of the stories and the rest of the time lay in Hasani's arms. I guess our secret was out now as glances were coming from all directions in ours. But I didn't care, it wasn't a secret to me, and Hasani seemed happy. At least, we didn't have to hide now. We could be open with our love for one another. We held each other closely and she played with my hair as I recovered from the concussion. First day staying at camp with nothing to do. It was boring, to say the least, but at least I had her and that's all that mattered.

It wasn't long before I was sleeping soundly only to awake the following morning. I watched Hasani as she dreamt. She looked so peaceful; eyes closed but fluttering as she reasoned. She was beautiful and I, so lucky to have her. My headache had subsided, and it would be there where the world was at peace laying in her arms that I would realise how truly lucky I was. To have found love in a world so full of wasted hate, to feel whole if only for a one-minute moment. My heart melted as she stroked my face and I knew that I was forever stolen.

The family had returned from their days' wanderings and I was once again enveloped with stories of their endeavours. Laughter arose from the camp giving it life. The moon shone brightly in the sky and once again I had fallen asleep.

I was awoken early by a kookaburra cackling in a nearby tree. Feeling better I arose and exited the rose bush to go for a swim in the lake. It was super early and only the watch was up.

"Hi, Kendall," I whispered gently as I passed her usual gum tree.

"Hey, Oda," came the same gentle whisper back.

I continued to walk down the path squinting at the morning sun as my body was not yet quite awake yet. Dropping my clothing on the way I didn't give myself the time to test the coolness of the water but shocked myself alive in one brisk dive. And it felt awesome. The water swirled around me giving me life, alleviating any of the forgone pressures of the days gone past. I floated seemingly weightless through the water buoyancy keeping me afloat as I played with the sunlight on my face. It was a glorious day. Soon I could hear footsteps nearby, awaking me from my fantasy. Alas, it was Charlie. He must have awoken with the same idea. We waded in the shallows for some time not saying much. He would open his mouth to silence then shut it again just as quickly.

"Well, get it out, Charlie." I beckoned.

"How long?"

"How long what?"

"How long have you and Hasani been, well, you know?"

"Oh, um, a little while. It just never really came up in conversation I suppose."

He beckoned for more, but it was then that I returned to my inner musings.

My soul was exposed and within me, I felt the warmth of what was. It electrified me and exhausted me all at once. My inner subconscious wanted me to persevere but I was at a standstill. My heart beat erratically within my chest and the pangs became so real. Like life itself was tormenting me. I looked to my internal locus of control and realised the depths of it all. So deep that, in fact, I could not control it. Never had I been able to even if for just moments in time I kid myself that I was in fact in control. But it was all a façade, one in which I had lived my life in this new world. If I were to tell the truth, then the only thing that kept me from falling further down the rabbit hole was love itself, the conqueror of all. It existed to allow me to feel something more than myself, to engulf my heart and soul in a magnitude so beyond my comprehension and I warmed in honour of it. It brought about a natural understanding that within this world there was hope. Hope for a future and a plan beyond that which was the everyday. And I yearned for it. A constant begging of my heart as it unravelled before my eyes and consciously, I was able to live. Luck, the word I live by thus had got me this far.

I moved to the water's edge and allowed the sun to bake me until I was well dry. Putting my clothes back on I made my way back to camp and decided to take it easy for the day. It was time to spend it with Hasani. We walked to a nearby town, the abandoned one covered in encroaching nature. I found a bathroom and tested it for water. Crystal clear, it flowed, and I ran a bath. The perfect place to escape. I on my back felt the cool of the water on the soft sides of my breast. It swirled around them knowingly as I bathed myself in soap I had found in a nearby cupboard. The suds stopped for a moment on my nipples and rested on the water surrounding them. The warmth continued downwards to my nether regions creating a lightness in me. It wasn't long before I was covered in suds, relishing in the content pool around me. On my back, I breathed in the relaxation allowing myself to transcend. My long brown locks were covered in the depths and I sighed but the sigh was that of contemplation. I was content in knowing that the life surrounding me was as it should be, and I felt a sense of belonging. Happiness. The water melting my soul, allowed my olive skin to be rejuvenated in its temperateness.

Hasani entered, a calm sense of being with a sexy tone in her walk. She crossed the threshold of the bath rearranging what was there to allow for two to become one. She smiled knowingly and we began to chat. Her body lathered, softening; smooth. She allowed herself to be cleansed by me, her suppleness absorbing that which was handed to her. The moisture of the water playfully caressed her fair skin.

We gazed into each other's eyes allowing for what was to become to sink in. With lust in my eyes, I questioned Hasani, she questioned back, and it wasn't long before she lay on top of me caressing my breasts, kissing me passionately. Intensely, she shifted to playing with the entrance to my vagina. And with one swift movement, she was inside of me. I gasped with the pleasure of it. Again, she retreated and entered with even more intent. It was smooth and breath taking. She beckoned, "Get out of the bath." I was in a state of ecstasy. Too involved to fully fathom what she was asking as once again she retreated and entered again. "Get out of the bath." Knowingly I climbed out of the bath and we were laying on the floor before I knew it. I was insatiable. Hasani pinned me on my back and with quick thrusts entered me. I couldn't help but let out moans as the feeling became unbearable. She quickened her pace, stopping only to pressure my G-spot, giving me even more of a reason to beg. I was in a state of bliss and quickly came to my peak.

We moved to a nearby bedroom and played in the 69 position. Allowing each other to lick and feel inside. I felt as though we were one. I pulled Hasani on top of me. Entering her as I did so. She pulled back and entered me from behind, but it got the better of her. She moved from on top and pushed me further on my back. Again, penetrated me so deeply that the world around me was forgotten. Naturally, I was engulfed in a state of ecstasy. She continued intently penetrating me deeply then moving in short sharp thrusts continued to make me wetter. I couldn't help but come and my head was once again transcended to that place where I was in a trance. We lay in each other's arms gently caressing each other. As I walked out of the house, I found a book. It read, *Inner Musings*. It was a book of something called poetry. I read the first one aloud.

'Time is the only valuable thing that we have, without it the people around us can no longer be together. To think that life is endless and can be immortalised is the greatest lie that the system taught us. That we can live in peace and love with those dearest to us. We don't get to choose our time and the world around us has failed us; it does not allow us to fulfil our destinies but only allows for us to feel a false sense of security in this lifetime. The cards were dealt well before we were even born, and this is the only factor that allows or disallows us from living to the greatest of our potentials. It is only that the circumstances and people around us that change our paths; that blacken or lighten our souls and poisons or enlightens our minds. But without light there is only darkness

The part that really hit me was that my life was supposedly all part of a predisposition. That whatever lay before me had already been. I thought about this all the way back to base camp. It was a slow walk back and we held hands as we trekked. I thought about the possibility of being the master of my own fate. Of the many pathways that can happen with each decision made. That maybe I was not predestined to have one life but many. The nature around me caught my attention and I kept silent the whole way back. I felt at peace.

Once again this would not last long. "Oda, hurry, get to camp." Came Kendall. "We have sighted a large group of Razors and they're heading our way."

"Fuck," I responded and quickly crept under the rose bushes to safety.

We heard them trek past us, words that could not be made out but sure enough they were Razors and once again on the scout. "How many?" I queried Kendall.

"At least a dozen."

Big group. I wondered what they were doing so far out but if this was the scouting group then the camp itself must have had at least 50 Razors in it. Too big for us to risk it. We made a plan to try and find their camp that night, to see how close they were and whether they were camped for the long haul.

Chapter 21

When night fell Kendall, Sam, Tom and I sorted our packs and headed out to scout the area. It wasn't long before we saw the smoke. Hiding in a nearby tree we looked over the camp. Luckily enough, we hadn't run into any scouts and were free to see how big the camp was. And it was big. There was a whole encampment, large too. They looked like they were camped in for a while, right near the lake too. We retreated just as silently as they had come.

"We have been lucky so far, but it looks like our luck's run out." Kendall supposed.

Sam and Tom went to tell the other crew and we sat contemplating what to do next. Our main supply area had been cut off. We were smart enough to have some food stored up, but we knew it wouldn't last long. So, our only option was to keep watch over the encampment over the following days. We moved back and forwards, making sure to cover our tracks and keep away from the scouts; who were becoming more and more evident. On the third day of one of our routine scout trips, I noticed something different within the camp. This was no ordinary camp and then I saw him. It was Kemp. No wonder the site was so big. It made sense to me. Which also meant that Chase was probably leading one of the scout groups. I started to hyperventilate as I stood there, drawing attention to myself. Sam tried to calm me, but the anxiety attack took over and I was gulping for air in no time. Sam grabbed me and motioned to the others to stand watch as I with vague intent was extrapolated from the outskirts of camp. We made it back to base, but I was shivering something solid. Hasani held me close as I worked my way through the motions of a panic attack. I seriously thought I was going to die; anything was better than getting caught again.

The camp was abuzz with plans and the other group had come to join us as they nutted out a strategy; a plan to get supplies and food for the upcoming weeks. I heard Charlie mentioning that we head west to hunt and keep well away from the main camp. Tried to stay as stealthy as possible and to only take small games so as not to draw attention to ourselves. I was happy if I wasn't anywhere near Kemp.

The next few days were a blur as I contemplated what this meant for me. How I was going to get through this so that I could contribute but it would come naturally; I couldn't force these things. For now, Hasani would take my place and hunt for food.

It was like any other afternoon when it happened. Sam came sliding into camp covered in blood. "They've got them," he yelled.

"Got who," I questioned back.

"They took Charlie and Hasani."

My heart stopped in my chest. I sprang into life. "What the fuck happened?"

"They came from all around us. We had lined up some game and Charlie was just about to bag it when they came at us. I managed to fend off a few of them, but Hasani and

Charlie had no chance. They had guns on them. I had to fight my way through to escape. Fucken scouts."

I was pacing now. I knew that I shouldn't have let her out there. Fuck!

I grabbed my nearest weapon, an AK and proceeded to exit the rose bushes. The only problem is that Sam caught me by the shoulder. "You can't."

"I can and I will."

"Think about it, Oda. We need a plan. You can't let your emotions take over now. You'll get us all caught."

I was so unclear about it all, I just wanted to rescue her, to get her out of the clutches of those Razor bastards, my head was so foggy with rage and clear with intent. I didn't realise that in my haste I could get everyone killed and to be quite frank I didn't care; all I could think about was Hasani. But Sam was right, we needed a plan and a good one at that. In scouting the camp, the days before we knew where most things were located and where most people were situated but we still had no idea of their routines. To make it more difficult, the scouts were forever moving so it was hard to gauge where they would be. Obviously, the first thing to do was to locate the scouts and work our way in from there. I drew on my knowledge of flora and had an idea to concoct a potion out of the highly poisonous Christmas Rose. With the reasoning of putting it into the communal cauldron and poisoning the camp but the problem was getting to the cauldron. We would have to enlist one of the slaves and that was dangerous because we were yet to know the differences between all of the people within the camp.

I put the AK on the corner of the cave wall and wedged myself up within a small crevice. The foetal position seemed all that could keep me from jumping out of my skin and crying all at once. I tried to block out all of the scenarios of what could be happening out of my head. Pushing my hands to my temples I physically tried to push them away, but they continued to intrude. I was so unaware of myself that tears had started to fall from my eyes and my heart began to feel like it was being wrenched from its fissure. Throw me a bone was all I could think, think fucken hard, how was I going to get her back? I needed to get out, so I picked up the AK and remembered a patch of Christmas Roses I had seen to the north. I bundled a pack and took a switchblade and not without resistance I journeyed through the forest. Memories kept flooding my thoughts. Her smiling face, the way she flicked her hair in the day's sun, the kind words she spoke to me. They engulfed me which made my plight even more compact. I pushed through Lantana and walked through the fields of daisies we used to make love in. It would be noon before I reached the site. And it was there I saw the irony in such beauty. I picked as much as I could fit in my pack and found a stream to settle in by. It was a trickle but still enough to recharge my energy, refocus my mind. Logic kicked in as all my emotions began to dissipate, all but one; anger. But through this came clarity of thought. Link in, find a slave, to pour the concoction into the cauldron. Take out the scouts one by one. Get into the camp, it all began to form in my mind and at this site our plan was formed.

By the time I had returned, it was nightfall and the rest of the camp was already in full swing, it seemed that Sam had already formulated his own plan and it was to begin tonight. It would be all of us involved this time – no one left behind. Guns, bows and knives were being distributed and it seemed that finally all of our practice would come to fruition. I worked on the potion, carefully extracting the poison from the plant and mixed it in the clear water I had obtained from the stream. Sam assembled a team of six – Rudy, Steve, Kendall, Robert, Simone and himself were to pick off the scouts while Robert and Sally found someone to put the poison in the cauldron. Jack, Cameron, Mae and Sandy were to start working on setting up a perimeter in case anything went wrong, they were the first line of defence within the camp. They were to station nearby the tents until joined by Sam's crew. I had one mission, find Hasani and get her out. But in order to do that I joined Sam's team to help rid of the scouts. The plan was by dawn the scouts would have been taken care of and the morning meal would contain the poison.

The sun had completely faded by the time we were ready to move out. Stealth was the name of the game as we tramped through the forest towards the camp. This would be no easy feat but when it comes to matters of the heart all the chips were down. I had an extra bit of motivational anger which set a fire in my soul and nothing would get between Hasani and I, nothing.

Sam led as the moon lit our way. The southern cross gave us a beacon to light our way. As we approached the lake the area became less dense and we needed to tread more carefully. Suddenly Sam stopped dead in his tracks. It was moments before he motioned for us to sit still and retreated into the night. The next thing I heard was a low moan and a simple crack. He returned. "One down." How he saw him I still don't know. It was as if he appeared out of nowhere, but Sam was an expert and I was glad to have him on our team. We stepped forward making a circular movement around the lake. If only the night would be this easy.

Again, he motioned and looking up into the trees I could see two scouts. Both were on point, looking lively but they had not seen us through the thicket yet. Sam signalled to move in a circle. We had practised this scenario out in the forest. First would come the bow and arrows and second the assault on the ground. Simone and Steve pulled back tightly on their bows and released, both scouts fell from the trees and landed with a thud. Sam, Kendall, Robert and I were on them within seconds. Slitting their throats, and dragging them into the thicket, we moved further around the lake.

In an instant there was a troop of at least four scouts heading our way, they must have been doing their routine perimeter search. We spread out again and Sam and Simone moved in from the back of the pack. The first two were easy. They were so taken by surprise that the cuts to their throats didn't allow for even an exhale. The two in the front turned with the scuffle and that's when Steve and Rudy stepped in behind them grasping them in sleeper holds. It was a lot more noise than necessary, but it was the lesser of two evils in this case. We dragged the bodies behind a nearby oak and some lantana trees. It was then we heard the gentle crack of sticks behind us. "Put your hands up," came a steady manly voice from behind. At this point, Sam edged his way into the lantana beside me. He was hidden by the large oak tree. We dropped our weapons and did as we were told. He edged in further and with one breath he went to send the call out but not before Sam had covered his mouth and snapped his neck in one swift movement. It was then I noticed that I hadn't had a single breath and gasping for air I let out a sigh of relief.

We continued to circle. By now, Robert and Sally would have found a slave and the others would be positioned behind the tents. Well, here was hoping anyway. As we rounded the bend onto the field in front of us there was a large pack of scouts talking loudly 5 of them in total. We decided to move through the thicket and create a small scene just off into the dense bush. Draw them in. It was too risky to go out into the open. So, we threw some rocks at a nearby tree. Subtle enough to stir them but not enough to alarm them. Immediately, they turned to the noise and circled around it, now the numbers were much fairer. I eyed off the scout closest to me. A tall man with a long beard, medium framed, the shadows disguised the rest of him. This would not be easy. As he rounded the closest tree I stealth out and climbed on his back trying to hold him in a sleeper hold. But he was so tall I caught him around the shoulders. He turned abruptly and hit me with the butt of his gun, I turned slightly so that it caught me on the shoulder. I raised my gun at him, and he looked at me with a wry smile. "You know how to use that girly?"

"Sure do, and I'm not afraid to either." Knowing I couldn't because it would be too noisy, I waited for him to drop his gun and it was then the duel began. I pulled my knife and swung wildly at him. He toyed with me for a while and then drew his knife. We circled intently moving our bodies into different positions as the circle changed. I swung at him only to find the crisp clear air and he pulled my arm towards him pulling me into a chokehold. I quickly swung his arm over my head as I kicked back into his groin. He grunted and doubled over so I had time to move in behind him and quickly slit his throat. I was hoping that all of the others that I would come into contact with would be that easy, but I knew better.

It was then I looked up to see nothingness, it was fair to say we had definitely chosen the right tactic here. The others circled around me and we stood still waiting to see if any others had heard. It would be moments before we made our next move. Moving slowly through the trees we found more scouts hiding amongst a thicket and in a tree. The trees would be harder. Sam made a quick movement of the scout in the thicket and cloaked in his clothing he moved towards the next scout. Head down he climbed towards him. The scout in the tree made conversation but they were only low groans from where I was standing. I could see his face though and it wasn't until Sam was right on top of him did a face of realisation search him. He was done in seconds. We moved even more gracefully through the thicket making sure only to make the necessary sounds as a tree branched snapped below or leaves from the fallen debris crunched underfoot.

Now we were on the outskirts of the camp. There were sure to be more scouts out there so Steve, Simone, Rudy, Robert and Kendall were given the mission of finding more of the scouts. It would be Sam and I who would venture into camp to find Hasani. Sam motioned me forth and it was then I knew that I was about to encounter my greatest fear. My legs swayed beneath me and I caught Sam on the shoulder. He motioned towards me, I waved back steadying myself. We moved forward together into the early hours of the morning. Without the scouts, it was easy enough to move around the shadows of the campsite. We looked for manned tents and targeted them first. There were only three of them so I thought that this would be easy enough. Rounding the first tent I saw two shapes. One each. This would have to be silent. This time I chose the smaller of the two and had him choked out on the floor in one swift move. We stood for a moment before entering the tent. Supplies. Nothing but supplies. But there were a few knives, so I pocketed two blades and we moved on to the next tent. It was more lit here, so we needed to create a distraction. Sam in his newfound clothes became bait and he called quietly to the two men at the tent's face. "Over here, I hear something in the bushes." They took it and with knives at the ready followed Sam into the thickets behind. I heard some low groans and a scuffle and Sam emerged unscathed smiling at me through the darkness. This time I lifted the tent nearing the back corner to see what was inside. There were definitely sleeping bodies and what looked like a cage. "I think this is it," I whispered to Sam. We moved to the front and opened the flaps of the tent with care. Intently we circled the inside of the tent. There were three bodies in the bed near the rear and a shape curled up in the corner of the cage. Sam moved to the bodies on the bed and I moved to the cage. "Hasani," I whispered. The figure stirred slightly. "Hasani, is that you?" A pair of eyes gleamed back at me. The form moved towards me.

"Who is it?" a woman's voice, Hasani's voice, came back to me.

"Oh my god, it is you. Quick, we need to get you out of here." The bodies on the bed began to stir and we stilled like rabbits in torchlights. Sam leaned further into the side of the tent his weapon trained on the bodies. I moved stealthily towards the door to the cage, but it was padlocked. There was no way I was getting through this without a sound. Sam's eyes said it all as they widened, and the bodies stirred on the bed. As the demon moved onto his side, I saw a glimmer of a key in the night's light. I motioned towards it and Sam returned knowingly. His face was partly covered by the shadows, but I knew it was him. I began to shake and had to mentally assert myself to pull it together. The light was advancing quickly outside, and we had lazily left the tent partly open, so much that the bodies on the bed began to stir even more. "Out, out." Came HIS voice. It was Kemp. The two others as commanded went to leave immediately but not before getting a glimpse of Sam against the tent. They gasped in unison. Sam trained his weapon on them and shook his head. "Now I said, now." Came Kemp's voice again. Even more urgently Sam shook his head and it was then Kemp sat up. His face was now lit by the slithers of sunlight before it. He realised immediately and warned. "One shout and you're done for."

"One bullet and you're done for," Sam retaliated.

They were caught in a standoff. Sam commanded, "You two, in the corner. Not a sound or I'll put a bullet in each of you." They did as commanded moving to the corner hugging each other in fear. They would be no threat, but it was not worth the risk. Kemp had not seen me yet as he was facing Sam, luckily too as I was frozen in fear. "What do you want?" Sam did not reply. "Well, come on?"

"I want the key and the girl." It was then that he turned to see me kneeling by the cage. His face turned from almost bored to a sardonic smile. "Oda. I can't even imagine." Still frozen I stared back at him. Then with the realisation, he put it together. "Oh, she's yours. Well, what a find I have and what a position you're in. You'll never make it out of here."

Sam tuned in and placed the point of the rifle on Kemp's head. Without breaking away from me he pulled the necklace from its foundations. "Here." But as he moved to give it to Sam, Kemp grabbed the end of the butt of the gun and pulled it towards him. Sam had sense enough not to let it go off but was off balance for a moment before connecting his fist with Kemp's face. Kemp parted with the gun but was now aware that it was useless in this sense and Sam in this revelation came in with a second swing. The key fell from his hand and shot across the floor. They wrestled on the bed, but I was too preoccupied with the key to think anything of it. I sprang into action, racing across the floor to where it lay. The girls sat dormant in the corner; I would imagine too scared to move. In one swift motion, I grabbed the key and returned to the cell.

"I've got you, Hasani, just one minute." It was then I heard a prevalent 'snap' and turned just in time to see the morning sun catch the eyes of Sam, there was nothingness in them, and his body was limp. I opened the cell but was not quick enough as a towering Kemp lay his fist into the side of my head. Stars gathered in my eyes and I struggled to stand. He grabbed me and threw me onto the bed behind me. Disorientated I tried to find the way up, but he was upon me. Grabbing my arms, he pinned me to the bed, Sam lying dead beside me. I struggled, pushing my hips towards his, trying to knock him off balance but it was no use he was too strong, it had always been that way. Out of the corner of my eye I could see Hasani moving to strike Kemp. I was too late; Hasani didn't escape, and before I knew it, she was laying slumped on the floor. "Fuck you, Kemp, fuck you," I yelled and struggled even harder. He grabbed my shirt and ripped it from my body.

"You little fucker," he yelled into my face, "Nothing but fucken trouble." He continued to tear at my bra releasing it with one pull from its front freeing my breasts. "I've been waiting for this for a long fucken time." His naked body pushed against mine, his chest holding down firm upon my breasts as he reached for my cargo pants buttons. "Just you fucken wait." He pulled them loose and started to rip my pants from my body. I was enraged and threw myself around trying to get free. But it was no use. He pushed me in a violent thrust onto my front and held me in a lock. I felt the breath release from me as I was searching for air. I was naked before him and could feel him growing bigger on my backside. "You little bitch." He turned me to face him and I gasped for air. Holding my throat, I moved my hands to his, he widened my legs and with one quick thrust, he was inside of me. More violent thrusts followed as he scowled at me. His spits hit my face as he forcefully invaded my body. I swung my head wildly from side to side to try and free myself from his hateful gaze. He penetrated me even more deeply and I groaned with discontent. The words came more easily now. "Fuck you, Kemp, fuck you." But with each word, he forced harder and faster. I could hear Hasani starting to cry from the corner and the beginnings of the camp were rising with the waking of the sun. His groans were prevalent now as he continued to fuck me, hard and fast. He slapped his body against mine so aggressively that I could feel the bruises rising from beneath the surface of my skin. I gasped for air as he tightened his grip around my throat. He quickened again and with one loud groan, he released inside of me.

He released my throat and I gasped for air. Doubled over I tried to rise but my head was too faint, I fell to the floor. He opened the cage and threw me and Hasani inside. "You and your whore stay put." Hasani grabbed a hold of me and in her arms, I felt safe to regain my consciousness. Kemp was pacing now. Not hiding his anger, he threw a canister from a nearby table across the room and in his rage upended a nearby table. "Get out!" he screamed at the girls who immediately left his presence. Shifting in his motive he lunged towards the cage and struck it with his hands, he stared directly into my eyes. I retreated further into Hasani's arms. He lifted his head and left the tent without a word. Outside, I could hear cries from the campsite as the murderer had been found and then Kemp's call going out, "Secure the camp."

I was shaking now, the adrenaline wearing off, and I grew closer to Hasani my cheek on her cheek. I felt warm, loved, at home. "Hasani, I love you." It came freely. It was then I heard a familiar voice outside, it was Chase. My brother who I had not seen in what felt like years. A feeling of satisfaction came over me. I do not know if it was because of the gentleness I could still sense in his voice or the fact that I thought that he would be dead by now and here he was standing there in the flesh. I moved to hear him further. They were discussing the perimeter and Kemp was ordering him to stay close to camp but to get his troops to circle the boundary and find the infidels. "Go." And with that he was gone again. I was certain of one thing, if Chase was on task then the others didn't have a fighting chance. Kemp came back through the tent's threshold. He spoke, "And what am I going to do with you?" He was talking about Hasani. "We can't have you distracting Oda now, can we? I have bigger plans for her now." I grabbed hold of her in my fright. What was he going to do? "Remember Rose?" How could I forget? "Maybe I should burn her at the stake. Give her to another leader? Watch her stumble into the bushes while I shoot her with an arrow right through the heart? No, that would be too easy. You need to suffer. Suffer like I have all these months without you. Then maybe, you will understand the pain I have been in."

He went suddenly and it was just Hasani and I left to ourselves. "We need to get you out of here." I tried the lock on the cage, but it was to no avail. "Hasani, listen to me, we need to get out, now." Hasani didn't move. She looked almost paralysed. I heard a scurry outside and yelling from the camp. It seems that they had found some of our group. I couldn't see them, but I could hear the violent abuse being yelled at them. "On your knees bastard," came a command and then a gunshot rang out. My heart quickened its pace. I leaned into the door of the cage to try and sneak a peek through the slither of light flowing through the tent's flaps. Someone was laying on the ground, a pool of blood surrounding them. He was facing away from me, but I knew it was one of ours. Then two others. Kendall and Steve, their heads pulled back by their scruffs. "Where are the others?" but they were silent. Then came the assault. A boot into Steve's stomach and the butt of a gun into Kendall's head. "Where the fuck are they? How many of them? You answer me or the end of this gun will be the last thing you ever see." They were still silent and one of the men turned to shoot Kendall in the face. "Stop." It was Kemp. "We've got time. They can't be too far away, let the scouts do their job and tie these two up." He was gruff with his words, almost impatient. Kendall and Steve were taken out of view. Kemp was wandering around deep in thought. I'd never seen him like this before so somewhat indecisive. "Bring them out." He ordered two men to get us.

They were quick to respond and were soon upon us. I grabbed Hasani with one hand and the crate with the other. But it was no use, they were a lot stronger than both of us. The taller one grabbed a hold of my hair and pulled me from the cage. While Hasani was dragged out feet first. I struggled against the man, he got me into a lock and pushed me forward, out of the tent. "Tie them up." The ropes were tight against my arms and my legs were strangled but it didn't stop me from fighting. We were now exposed to the whole camp surrounding us. He put it to the crowd, "What should we do with her?" He pointed at Hasani. A string of cries came out from the crowd.

"I know what I would do with her."

"Give her the royal treatment."

"Kill her slowly."

"Maybe I should leave her to them." He pointed, speaking directly to me and I could feel the thirst of the camp.

He moved behind Hasani and held a knife to her throat. "Perhaps, blood is what you want. Maybe I'll give it to you." He stabbed her in the chest. One quick blow. She doubled over and I couldn't help but yelp. It was no use begging, Kemp was wild. I grabbed at her, but my captor held me tight, pulling my head back. Blood started to trickle from the wound. It was shallow but enough to cause the pain he had intended. "Get me some more rope," he commanded. His allies responded and passed it to Kemp. He tied it into the form of a noose and suspended it from a nearby tree. Cheers rung out from the camp. He took Hasani and placed her head inside of the noose. Then suspended her from the tree. Hasani struggled for breath in the air and then he let her down, only to soon repeat the process. An ache sprung out from my heart and I writhed to get free. But my imprisoner had a firm grip on me. I was helpless. Helpless to support the woman I loved. Three more times he suspended her and then dropped her to the ground. She gasped for air lying in the dirt. He grabbed her and threw her into the dust. I looked up to see Chase watching from the shadows of the tree line. My eyes searched his and he turned away as quickly as I had looked up. I felt helpless and an anger was starting to boil inside of me. Kemp picked up Hasani and held her. He whispered something in her ear and then took her to a nearby tree. There he tied her. "All yours, boys." He looked at me with his wry smile. I was cursing now, arching my body to try and get free. They swarmed on her and were quick to rape her. I again searched Chase. But it was no use, he wasn't there anymore. I closed my eyes and all I could hear were the whimpers coming from Hasani. In my mind, I heard a familiar tune. It was that of my mothers. She used to sing it to us as kids. I felt it rise within me and I found myself singing to Hasani.

Love is gentle,

Love is kind,

Love will stir your heart and mind.

And if you let your light shine through,

Love will guide you to the truth.

She stopped to listen, and I could tell that it was carrying her away. My voice. The rapists stopped for a moment observing Kemp to see what he would do. Kemp had his eyes trained on me. I kept singing aware of my surroundings but encapsulated in visions of memories gone past. I beckoned that this would not be the last memories I have of Hasani. The song grew inside of me and I got louder. Kemp came to my side and soon enough I heard a voice.

Chapter 22

"Tell them to stop." It was firm and forceful. It came again. "Tell them to stop or I'll shoot you dead."

Kemp's voice came then almost knowingly. "Move away from her." They were quick to respond. I opened my eyes to see Chase standing behind Kemp with a gun to his head. "Give her to me." There was a pause then Chase again. "Now!" They untied her and released her to him. "And Oda."

It was then Kemp responded, "No, not Oda. You can take the other one, traitor, but there is no way that I am giving up, Oda." He forced the gun to Kemp's head. "You do as I say, or my face will be the last thing that you ever see." Hasani was by Chase's side and Kemp was ropable. He grunted then finally retracted his words. "Fine, take that bitch." He nodded and I was released into Chase's care.

"Both of you get dressed and get behind me." He spoke gently to me. I followed finding some clothes in a nearby tent. I wanted to take the gun right out of Chase's hands and kill Kemp then and there. It would be over then. But Chase continued to walk us slowly backwards towards the thicket his gun trained on Kemp. Kemp started to walk towards us and at this point, he was eerily quiet. Chase beckoned him closer. "You're coming with us." He motioned for Kemp to come forward. And with the gun trained at him Kemp did as he was told. His face was contorted with rage. "Walk," Chase commanded. And with that, he walked a few paces in front of us. We briskly walked out of the camp and headed towards the morning sun. Chase must have known these woods just as well as me, so he rounded us to a nearby opening. "They will be following us," he spoke. "They will kill us if they catch us." He was tying Kemp's hands together and binding him to a nearby tree using rope from his satchel. "My scouts are trained well."

"You've risked everything for us," I stammered. Kemp was struggling against the ropes, so Chase trained his weapon on him. "Why would you do that?"

"I can't really explain it. It's like I just snapped out of it. Like I was awoken from a dream. When I heard that, that song you sang. The one our mother used to sing to us as children. I felt a rising inside of me and my emotion took over. All that had been numbed before came to life and I realised that this was my chance. To redeem myself."

Kemp store at Chase in an effort to draw him in. It had been the ultimate betrayal and Kemp's rage grew. "Get me out of these bindings so help me God I will gouge out your eyes one by one and rip off your balls."

Chase ignored Kemp which only infuriated him more. "They will come looking and when they do, I will show no mercy. You have no way out, Chase. If you give up now, I may think about a quick death rather than the one I have planned for you. You do not know pain like the kind that I will give you." Chase disregarded Kemp further and gestured for us to keep moving. He untied Kemp from the tree and Kemp struggled wildly against him, but it was to no avail as

Chase was now a well-built man and held him easily in his grasp. "Come on now, we need to keep moving." I heard a rustle in the bushes not far off behind me and knew they were onto our scent.

We walked for days, entering rivers and climbing through dense rainforest in order to cover our tracks. There were no signs of the scouts but that's how they worked, most stealthily in the trees and surrounding bushland. Chase seemed confident that they were far behind and exposed us to a lair he had found on his previous scouting trips. There was a tight crevice in a gap between two rocks, barely enough room for one person to squeeze through, we ventured in single file. The gap opened up into a vast area covered in dirt. It was surrounded by rocks but there was another smaller space at the other end that if need be could become an exit. The sun was setting, and Chase pulled some berries and nuts from his rucksack, "Eat," he coerced. "You'll need your strength." We sat in silence none of us able to sleep at first. Chase took the first watch. I lay in Hasani's arms and she was propped up against a rock. The sandman took me soon enough and I was asleep fatigued by all of the last day's stressors. It was morning when I woke and Chase and Hasani were busy chatting in an adjacent corner. Kemp was still trained on Chase. My belly was rumbling as the days of not eating much had caught up with me. But it seemed that Hasani was a step ahead of me. Chase was going to give me the gun to watch over Kemp and head out to find food. I argued profusely but it was no use as inevitably Hasani and I did not have the strength to scavenge right now so we sat and kept watch. "If I'm not back by noon, kill him and find a safe spot to hide." I had just got my brother back, there was no way I was leaving him now. But I responded with the answer he wanted, "Sure." What else was I to do, we had Kemp and there was no way I was letting him go.

As soon as Chase had left the verbal assault started. "You will never get away with this. My scouts will find you and I will gut her like a fish right in front of your eyes. You will know pain then and I will keep you locked up until your dying days." I ripped the sleeve off of my shirt and gagged him. It's not that it was affecting me as much as it was annoying me. Through muffled groans, he tried to assault me further, but I had eyes for Hasani and soon blocked him out. I moved to kiss her, but she backed away. "Not now." She looked at Kemp and went white with fear.

"It's okay. He is dead to me." But it did not matter, she had been to places that I would never know and there was no returning presently from there. I could understand to a certain edge but the degree to which she had been affected I did not know. Only that it was enough for her not to want to be placed in the same space as him.

Chase soon returned with some game and I remembered that I was ravenous. He set a fire by day and cooked the rabbits he had caught. We ate without cause and before long the darkness had set in. "We have to move on." Chase insisted. But this would not be easy. Kemp was struggling already. The gun trained at him wasn't as powerful of an ally to us tonight. Kemp was restless and not afraid to make our lives difficult. We ambled through the forest and up the side of a mountain, Kemp in tow. It was getting harder now as Kemp was fighting us, so Chase told Kemp to get to his knees, gave Hasani the gun and pulled me aside.

"We need to get rid of Kemp, now," Chase remarked motioning towards him. "He is becoming a liability."

"But what if the scouts find us?" I retorted worriedly.

"It's a gamble I know, but we can make more ground without him."

I thought for a while. Of course, I wanted to be rid of him. Shoot, I wanted to put him through as much pain as I had been through. To make him suffer. To relish every second of it. Because it was revenge, I wanted, wasn't it? But this needed to be quick, I knew we didn't have the time.

We turned to see Kemp pulling Hasani close to him. He had managed to work the ropes apart. Hasani still had the gun at this point and Chase yelled, "Throw the gun." She threw it but it landed only metres away. In the kafuffle Chase lunged forward and Kemp dove, both edging for the gun. Together they had a hand on it and were wrestling in the ferny undergrowth. Chase located the trigger point, pulled it and a shot rang out, but to no avail without the pointer he missed Kemp and hit a nearby tree. "Run." He yelled to Hasani and me. Surely the gunshot could be heard by nearby trackers I thought and quickly Hasani and I darted off into the undergrowth but not without a side of guilt for Chase. We ran as far as we could before our hearts gave out. At this point, I noticed the cliff face in the distance. With newfound hope I spoke, "This way." I pulled Hasani close to me and we ran through the lower part of the mountain until we got to our hiding spot, the cave in the lantana. It was then I spoke, "Are you OK?"

"I think so," came the response.

"What happened out there?"

"I don't know. I was standing there with the gun traced on him, and I turned to look at you and Chase for a minute second. I swear I didn't know he had undone the ropes. And he was on me in seconds."

She continued but my thoughts wandered to Chase. Was he OK? Were the scouts upon them? So many feelings were running through me. I couldn't help but wonder.

I finally spoke. "You stay here, it's safe here. I need to find my brother; I need to know he's OK."

The guilt had finally caught up to me. I was reluctant to follow through with it but, I had to know. Hasani beckoned to me, "Please stay, please don't leave me here." She was convincing in her motions, but Chase was my brother, the only blood I had left. I couldn't leave him and Hasani was safe in the cave.

I waited to recover then set off when morning broke to see if he was OK. I would then know if he was dead or alive at least. We had no weapons left as all of them went out in the raid. So, I fashioned a makeshift spear out of a nearby branch and set off along the mountainside. As I neared the location, I quietly climbed an adjacent tree so I could see the site. I was right, there were Razors, and there were also the remains of coals dying in the daylight. They looked attentive with bows raised and guns in check, so I didn't go any closer. I couldn't see Chase or Kemp and I couldn't help but feel a dread rising inside of me. I retreated back to camp.

Hasani was startled when I came through the lantana and stood still. "What's up?" I started. But then I saw. We weren't alone. Out of the shadows came four men, all lusty and searching for blood. "What is this?" I tried to comprehend, and my emotions changed from dread to realisation.

"Hasani?" I questioned. And the betrayal overcame me. She went to say something but a nearby Razor clamped his hand over her mouth and she was gone. Overwhelmed I fell to my knees and dropped my spear. They were on me in seconds and I didn't resist.

Walking to our next destination, I was deep in thought. How had I missed it? To what depths will they go? I was in anguish. The love of my life outed me to the ones I hated most. How could she do that? Recognition came over me as I struggled with this. Really could she have done this?

We came to the new Razor campsite within the day and I was once again met with an overpowering sense of dread. Chase was there hanging by his legs from a nearby pine. He sighted me and like a fish led to its slaughter he writhed. Hasani was nowhere to be seen. The world was spinning around me, tears fell from my eyes as I comprehended all that had happened. Failure filled me. Thoughts consumed me. There was no escape. So many killed and for what? To end up back at the start but in a worse position. Roaring laughter broke me from my thoughts. The camp of Razors began to encroach upon me and the leader of it all, Kemp came close. Whispering he told me of words gone past. "You will never escape. My eyes are everywhere. You are mine." Bewildered I could do nothing but stare.

The Razor holding me threw me face-first into the dirt and I spat as my mouth filled with dust. Shock had filled me, and the world was silent through the onslaught. When I was awoken from this, I was once again in my solitary cage feeling more alone than ever. I sighed allowing my thoughts to consume me. Hasani wouldn't have, more of a question really, had I been betrayed? How could I have got everything so wrong? Staring up at the tent roof I tried to piece it together that was when I heard the cries of my brother. I grabbed at the cage, trying to find a release but I was overcome. Another cry. What were they doing to him? I found my voice through all of this and began yelling at the top of my lungs. It was a mixture of frustration and attention, but no one came to see. It seems their intentions were to torture Chase. To get some reprisal from this traitor and they were searching for blood.

Lowering myself to the ground, pulling my knees to my chest and covering my ears were all I could do to survive the screams. It was then I noticed the vial in my pocket. It was the Christmas Rose. I had forgotten all about it. My mind went into a trance as I sat mesmerised by the bottle. The potion to end it all. Not taken lightly I hadn't been so seduced by death since I was in the clutches of Kemp. I mean what had I to live for? Hasani was a deceiver. Chase would soon be dead. I couldn't live a life with Kemp anymore. I toyed with the vial spinning it between my fingers. The substance was tantalising. I moved my head in closely and eyed it carefully. I could see the bubbles shifting as I moved the element from end to end. It was too much for me. In the end, dying is a quarrel in itself. It is in the absence of fear that peace evolves and suddenly everything goes quiet allowing your mind to become a beacon of its inner subconsciousness. The pangs of the past are destroyed and in those moments the distant memories of love and life gone past evolve; childhood laughter, games once played in innocence, family bonding; the hugs from my mother and the words of wisdom from my father all imparted in days which seemed so very long ago; bonds that even in death can and will not be broken; for the mind is a powerful place and the essence of the soul. the only thing that contains the light in all of this darkness. The only inevitability of life is death but how that happens can in some instances be in our control. Existing only in how many fights we have left. The will to live through all of the altercations; and when your physical body is almost destroyed, and your mind is in disillusionment; your life is at its edge; it's nice to know that peace endures within our choice. But I couldn't, could I? I slowly undid the lid. Some of the potion dripped over my fingers and I eyed it intently tracing it as it fell from my fingertips and onto my leg. Not willing to waste one drop I caught the liquid falling, swiping what was left of it off of my leg and placed it into the bottle. Fingers at the ready I moved them to my lips. One drop and it would be swift.

Chapter 23

My fantasy ended when loud shouts came from beyond the tent. I pocketed the Christmas Rose just as Kemp's body filled the doorway with his shadow. I trembled at the sight of him and moved to the opposing corner of the cage. He yelled out commands to his tribe but did not leave his station. What the hell was going on out there? More shouting could be heard but it wasn't organised as per usual. These were shortly followed by expanses of explosions. I could see the fires through my tent wall, but Kemp didn't move only yelled orders further from his standing point. It seems they had a battle on their hands, but who would dare? Startled again by the explosions I crept even further into my corner. Kemp drew nearer. He unlocked the cage and attempted to drag me out. I both cowered and fought from my spot in the corner like a trapped defenceless animal. He climbed into the cage and pulled at my hair. It was painful but I did not allow it to stop me from holding tightly to the cage wall; it shifted slightly. "Come here you little bitch." Another explosion, nearer to our tent and flickers of flame roared nearby. "I will not lose you again." He grabbed me around the waist and pulled at my tightly linked fingers around the cage. One finger loosened, then another, it wasn't long before he had all of my fingers undone and he was pulling me out of the cage.

Whoever it was outside was edging close as the yelling neared. Kemp dragged me out of the tent and into the open. Here I could see more clearly now. It was chaos. Razors were running but it seemed without any real direction and Kemp started again yelling orders, "Smith, grab the chain." Smith ambled off in between the fire and the fighting and soon returned with it. Kemp attached me to him by my waist and soon I was being led around. Another explosion went off and I hit the ground, the loud sound ringing in my ears. Kemp grabbed me around the neck, lifted me onto my feet and we ran. I knew none of the invaders, they were wearing clothes much like mine; not uniforms like those of the Theodoris. Arrows were in flight and both Razors and the invaders were hard in battle. All but a few of the tents had been set alight. "Theo, Caelin, Transit!" came Kemp's voice, "Move out!" In between the shouts and shots, we scuffled out of the campsite and towards the base of the mountains but not without chasers. Three of his men surrounded Kemp and were shooting wildly behind us at the pursuers, moving only to keep up with us. We were travelling fast, even with me in tow.

Gunshots rang out beside us as we ran but Transit was close by shooting backwards as we sprinted. He was skilled, really skilled. Before long we were at the base of the mountain. I recognised the cliff face before us. We dodged left into the thicket and started up the mountain. I couldn't help but slip on the loose rocks before me and Kemp would straighten up and clench his jaw in disapproval. It wasn't long before we reached an opening in the valley and he stood still in the ferny undergrowth surrounding the clearing. Transit,

Ario and Caelin surrounded us with bows and guns at the ready. Kemp took a sidearm in his right hand and cupped a hand around my mouth. I was struggling to breathe at this point and took gulps of air under his hand. All went still. Whoever was following us must have seen the clearing and taken positions in the undergrowth. "Kemp!" An unfamiliar voice came. "We've got you surrounded." Then silence before, "Hand over the girl," The men traced their weapons in the bushes beyond but there wasn't a sound to be heard. Then it came again, closer this time but not before it ended, "Ke…" shots rang out in its direction. An arrow landed at Kemp's feet. "That was a warning shot, the next one won't be." The manly voice boomed from beyond. Kemp moved the gun from his side and pointed it directly at my head. He then took his hand from my mouth, unsheathed his dagger from its side brace and moved that to my throat.

"Kill me and I kill Oda. Come any closer and I kill Oda." Why was I his bargaining chip? I quivered in fear.

"No one wins here, Kemp," came the voice from the depths. "Let her go and we will let you go. Now lower your weapons."

It was a voice of authority but calm in its actions. The type a father would use but in a terrorist threat. I was confused. Who were these people and what did they want with me? Uncertainty came over me. Was I just going to another kind of jail? I was over being imprisoned and I straightened with this notion. Kemp tightened his elbow grip around my shoulder and slowly dug the knife into my neck deeper. I wondered, what he was contemplating. It seemed to me he didn't have many choices but for Kemp to give up power in a standoff? It was against his very vein. The voice came closer and a shot rang out piercing the tree the man was standing at. It was transit, to my left. Next thing an arrow pierced his upper thigh and he was doubled over in pain writhing on the ground. Other than the single grunt when the arrow went through, he had made no noise. These people whoever they were had been trained well, and the archer had extreme accuracy. "We don't want to be the catalyst for any more deaths, but if you force our hand, we will have to kill you, now let her go." It wasn't long before the voice came within metres of us and I could make out a form behind a thick eucalypt tree surrounded by the ferny vegetation. He seemed taller than most and his arm was thick with muscle. He was wearing a black singlet with blue jeans. "Kemp." How did he know Kemp? What did he want from me? The confusion overtook my observations as I tried to formulate some kind of reasoning. "Kemp. Tell your men to put their weapons down, we can do this in a way where nobody gets hurt." Kemp tightened against me, his raw chest muscles pulling into my back. He was sweating on me. Slow beads were forming on his arms, but his demeanour remained the same. "We've got you completely surrounded. Your camp is no doubt being disbanded right now. Your choice is the only thing keeping you alive at this point. Give us the girl." I felt a globule of blood trickle from my neck down to my clavicle, he was pushing hard.

Out of his silence came. "She is mine. Oda is mine. We are destined to be together forever. Back off or I kill her. In this world or the next, we will be together." His possession seemed to be only enhanced by this moment. He was not yet a rat in a cage in his mind but a bird in flight, for there seemed to be nothing else in this world he wanted more but me and there I was closest to him, even at that moment.

The mystery man gestured behind him and four more shadows filed in. They held handguns and they trained them on Ario, Transit, Caelin and Kemp. They kept a distance but circled around us. I could feel Kemp eyeing each of them off with a fierce gaze. "Kemp." His voice came again. It was then the light filtered through the trees onto his face. He was older, middle-aged perhaps and his face showed that of a man that had been through some really tough times. He kept his eyes on Kemp, blinking being his only break. "This is your final warning." And with more force in his voice, he specified, "Pass her slowly over to me." The man motioned forward with his arms.

Kemp took a deep breath and whispered in my ear, "You will always be mine." And with that, the knife dug deeper into my neck. The blood was flowing gently now. My shirt was filing with its intent. In one swift move, dropping the knife he spun me around and as I looked into his eyes, he began to choke me. Gunshots rang through and I was without breath. Every now and then Kemp would jerk backwards and forwards with the bullets entering his body, but he did not let go of his grip. He dropped to his knees and continued to look deep into my eyes. I was trying to gasp for air, but like a waterless goldfish, I had no response. It was all I could do not to stare into his eyes, this is the end, so introspectively I reflected; time is the only valuable thing that we have, without it the people around us can no longer be together. To think that life is endless and can be immortalised is the greatest lie that the system taught us. That we can live in peace and love with those dearest to us. We don't get to choose our time and the world around us has failed us; it does not allow us to fulfil our destinies but only allows us to feel a false sense of security in this lifetime. The cards were dealt well before we were even born, and this is the only factor that allows or disallows us from living to the greatest of our potential. It is only the circumstances and people around us that change our paths; that blacken or lighten our souls and poison or enlighten our minds. But without light there is only darkness and without enlightenment there is only darkness... again. Stars were beginning to fill my mind, limpness my body, and the fogginess took over.

I awoke, startled; gasping for breath I grabbed at my neck, but it was no longer entangled. The world around me was moving, I was moving and fast. Moments tracked past as I tried to gather my senses, and find my footing. It was dark and as my hearing adjusted, I could hear voices surrounding me. My eyes searched the darkness and soon locked on to one voice in particular. "She needs to rest. It's no use pushing her." I groaned into the deep as I found my voice. "It's OK," came the familiar voice, "Oda, rest."

"Who, who are you?" I mumbled. A torchlight flicked on and closest to me came the voice again.

"It's me, Alicia," came a sweet soft voice back.

She shifted and moved under my head where she played softly with my hair.

"Yes, it's me, darling. I'll explain later. For now, get some rest." Bewildered, I couldn't help but fall into a deep sleep.

I awoke to beeping noises around me. They got louder the more coherent I became. My eyes glazed at first but then gained focus on the roof above me. Where in the hell was I? The roof was white with cracks protruding through the paint. Lying on my back I moved my head to the left to the sound of the beeping. I winced as I focussed on my arm. A needle was pumping some fluid from a clear sack above me into my veins. A machine with moving green lines beeped. I sat up slowly. The room was clean; that was weird in comparison to my natural life. There was a door off to the right and a window lay before me. I was alone. Nothing in there but a lonesome black chair in the corner to my left and what I was laying on. It was then I realised, it was a bed, a real bed, not hay on the floor or a makeshift one, but one that had been fashioned in the old world. *This was the old world*, I thought and peered closer at the machine standing in front of me. As I gazed, I released the needle from my arm and suddenly a soft sound came from outside. It didn't take me long to realise that in taking out the needle I had set off an alarm. Panic came over me as I scrambled for the door, the grogginess hard to move through. It was locked. Footsteps were nearing my room and chatter filled the halls. Suddenly two women entered the room, "Take a seat." The first woman commanded. The second came into sight and it was my mother. Stumbling, I fell onto the bed. I tried to speak but I couldn't find the words to say.

Tears rolled down my cheeks as I started to cry. Whispering through now sobs I ached, "Mum."

"It's OK darling. Just listen to the lady here. She is here to make you feel better." Feeling dizzy, I laid back on the bed and allowed the lady to conduct her examination. She pointed lights in my eyes, felt my abdomen and checked my neck. She said something like my vitals were good and with a nod to my mother, she left the room.

It was her. It really was. I broke in, "But I thought… What happened?"

Over some time, she told me, after she was thrown into the forest and left for dead. She was found by a group of Wanderers who were travelling through the city. They nursed her back to health and took her here. Parts of it had been left whole in the war so the people who found her took her to this base. This particular building was a hospital in the old times. She explained that there are many people that live here now and that there has been ground gained in retaliation to the Theodoris. The Razors didn't tend to go to the cities so there is only one enemy here.

The resistance was fighting back? I was in shock. So many questions filled my mind. But the right timing would come. She came in for a hug, then gently spoke, "Please, come with me."

I whispered with one unresolved question, "Where's Kemp?"

Milton Keynes UK
Ingram Content Group UK Ltd.
UKHW020617281123
433366UK00014B/308